CANDICE
CARTY-WILLIAMS

KNIGHTS OF

Published by Knights Of

Knights Of Ltd, Registered Offices:
119 Marylebone Road, London, NW1 5PU

www.knightsof.media

First published 2021
001

Text copyright © Candice Carty-Williams, 2021

First published in the UK by Knights Of, 2021

The moral right of the author has been asserted.
Set in Charter
Design by Marssaié Jordan
Typeset by Laura Jones
Printed and bound in the UK

A CIP catalogue record for this book will be available from the
British Library

ISBN: PB: 978-1-913311-100
2 4 6 8 10 9 7 5 3 1

Empress & Aniya

Some of us are Empresses; those latchkey girls who are raising themselves, unknowingly desperate for the love they deserve but are too defensive to understand – or even receive – it.

And some of us are Aniyas. The girls who are raised with love, and are able to, in turn, give and show that love to those who don't know it.

This story is for the Empresses; you are loved.
And this story is for the Aniyas; we are grateful for you.

Chapter One

'Aniya, please can you actually *move over* and let Empress sit down, thank *you*?' Miss Tribble shouted across the classroom. She watched as Empress shuffled through the rows of desks and dropped her rucksack on the floor by the empty chair next to Aniya.

Without looking at Empress, Aniya – dark-skinned with black hair slicked back into a neat bun, slightly chubby and with a dimpled face that was often described as 'cute' – sighed and scooped her pens, hairbands, glasses and headphones over to her side of the double desk with her arm.

Satisfied that Aniya, who was one of the smartest in the class but could often be *quite* challenging, was going to let Empress actually have at least fifty per cent of the desk space, Miss Tribble turned back to the board and carried on explaining the exam schedule for the coming weeks.

Empress, brown-skinned and slim, with a face that was often described as 'older than its years', pulled the chair out and threw herself down on it. Her long black braids almost hit Aniya as she sat down. Slowly, she reached down to her bag and pulled out a pen she'd stolen from the newsagent and a battered notepad she'd found in a cupboard at home.

'Is that your actual notebook?' Aniya asked Empress.

Miss Tribble turned back to the girls. 'Actually, Aniya, if you could spend the first couple of days with Empress, that would be good. Thanks.'

'But Miss!' Aniya shouted. 'I don't know her!'

'But you will by the end of the week,' Miss Tribble replied. 'That's the point. Thanks again, Aniya.'

Aniya rolled her eyes before she could stop herself.

'You don't even know me,' Empress said quietly, still facing the board. 'Why are you being so rude?'

Aniya turned to look at the side of Empress's head and blinked slowly. She actually wasn't sure why she'd said that. Her mum always encouraged her to 'say a bit less'. *Maybe* this was one of those times, she thought.

'Well. I *don't* know you. I guess. So maybe I... I don't know, really,' Aniya spluttered. She wasn't used to being called out.

'I won't get in your way or anything,' Empress said. 'I can walk behind you for a bit just to figure out where everything is. I just need to know where I'm going. I don't need any friends.'

Aniya felt a bit embarrassed by the way she was being. She'd been feeling this way for a while, though. All these weird feelings, mainly confusion that came out as anger, jumping out without her realising. It had been going on for a few weeks. At first, she'd wanted to talk to her parents about it, but, when she went to say something to them, she got really angry at something small her mum had said in response instead and ended up storming off to her room. After that, she didn't bother bringing it up again.

'Everyone needs friends,' Aniya said.

'Not me. Just need to know where I'm going,' Empress repeated.

'Okay. Well. We'll see. What's your first class?'

Empress pulled the schedule she'd been given from the inside pocket of her blazer and scanned it with her eyes.

'Maths. Double.' Empress said. 'In block C, room... seven?'

'Oh, same as me!' Aniya smiled. 'Top set. Very impressive!'

'Why is that impressive?' Empress turned to Aniya to ask.

'Well, no, it's because...'

'You think cos I'm here on scholarship I'm not as smart as you?'

'I didn't say that!' Aniya spluttered. 'Don't be so defensive!'

'Well. You were thinking it.' Empress sighed as the bell went, signalling the end of form time. 'Let's go to maths, I guess. As I said, I'll walk behind you.'

* * * *

It was lunchtime and the canteen was *busy*. Empress had never seen anything like it. Kids sitting on tables, kids jumping over chairs.

4

This was meant to be a *private* school, she thought. She expected to walk in and see everyone sitting down reading while they ate, or whatever posh kids did. But nobody was really even eating, it was like everyone had just gathered in this large, old, dusty-looking hall to make as much noise as possible. She grabbed a grey plastic tray and stepped into the queue for food, while she carried on looking around the room. Empress liked to watch people more than she liked to talk to them.

She'd done enough people-watching by the time she got to the front of the queue to have understood who to avoid and who was harmless. She could see the people who were loners, the people who needed to be the centre of attention, and the people who actually were like the posh kids she'd imagined. They were the ones in the corner who would pause reading or writing to take a quick mouthful of food.

By the time the queue had moved forward, to the point that she was close to the menu and price list, she stopped people-watching and did some calculations in her head.

'What can I get you, darlin'?' The canteen server, a blonde woman who looked a little bit older than her mum and had kind green eyes, asked, jolting Empress out of her thoughts.

Empress knew that in the pocket of her blazer that had been itching her all morning, she had enough money for chips. Well, she had money for more, but if she bought more, it meant that she wouldn't have enough to eat for the rest of the week.

'Just a portion of chips please,' Empress said quietly, as she eyed the rest of the food on offer. It all looked incredible. The mashed potato looked creamy, the crunchy greens looked fresh, the salmon looked juicy, the chicken looked plump and crispy. Empress couldn't eat dairy, but she was even ready to risk it all for the stuff covered in cheese. She was so *hungry*. Her stomach felt like it was going to eat itself.

'Nothing else, darlin'?' The canteen server asked, spooning chips on to a plate. 'That's not enough to get you through the day!'

'I'm not a very big eater,' Empress lied, reaching out for the plate and putting it on the tray carefully. She just wanted the conversation to be over. She felt like people were listening and watching and she was already braced for new girl attention.

'Okay, well, I've given you some extra.'

'Thanks!' Empress took the plate and practically ran over to the till to pay for her food. She wanted this whole experience over and done with. She thought about how she would have rather just brought packed lunch and eaten it in the playground, but there wasn't any food in the house, so that was out of the question.

She kept her head down as she moved through the canteen. Not an easy thing to do when you're looking for somewhere to sit. Head still slightly bowed, she headed towards a quiet corner of the large and chaotic room.

She sat down by herself and started eating her chips. She put on her cheap headphones, connected her phone to the school WiFi and started listening to music to drown out the noise of everyone and everything.

She was sort of enjoying herself, lost in her own world, until a tap on the shoulder made her jump. She looked up and saw Miss Tribble standing over her.

'Eating by yourself, Empress?' Miss Tribble asked.

'Er,' Empress looked around at the empty table, 'yeah.'

'Well, that can't be very fun, can it?'

'It's fine.' Empress shrugged. 'I used to eat alone in my old school. I'm used to it.'

'Well, we can't have that,' Miss Tribble smiled. 'Where's Aniya?'

'I dunno!' Empress had no idea. She didn't care, either.

Miss Tribble pulled a chair out and sat next to Empress, who had to fight everything in herself not to ask her form tutor why she'd sat down.

'I know, I know, teachers are annoying and boring, I know. To you, yes we are. And don't worry, I'm not sitting down to have lunch with you,' Miss Tribble assured Empress. 'But look, coming to a new school is hard. And isolating yourself is much harder. And I know you're probably not doing it on purpose, but I put you and Aniya together for a reason. She's very kind and her heart is in the right place. She can be a bit… outspoken sometimes, but, you teenagers can't help it.'

Empress wondered when Miss Tribble was going to stop talking.

'Anyway,' Miss Tribble said. 'Just keep in mind what I said. You don't have to be alone, Empress.'

When Miss Tribble finally left, Empress thought about how much easier it had always been to be alone. Nobody let you down that way.

* * * *

The next day, Empress made her way through the assault course that was the canteen again. It was somehow even louder today.

'Empress!'

Empress almost dropped her tray at the sound of someone shouting her name across the canteen. She followed the direction of the voice and saw Aniya sitting with four of her friends at a table right in the middle of all the chaos. At the heart of the noise.

Empress did not want to walk into the centre of that. So, she nodded at Aniya and went to walk ahead.

'Empress, come and sit with us!' Aniya shouted.

'So, you want everyone in this school to know my name?' Empress sighed under her breath.

'Come, come!' Aniya smiled.

Empress took a deep breath and headed over, gripping her tray tight. She just wanted to be by herself.

'Okay, so this is who I was talking about. The new girl. My assigned friend. Miss Tribble said that I should look after her,' Aniya said when Empress arrived at the table. 'Sit down, sit down!'

Empress tried to figure out if Aniya could be trusted. She'd changed her tune from yesterday. Empress wondered if their form tutor had said something to her.

While she tried to work out Aniya's change of heart, she attempted to figure out where to sit. Two of the girls were sitting on the table and the other three were on chairs. Should she sit on the table and balance the tray on her lap, or just sit in the empty chair and put her tray on the table? Trying to figure out how to be in the first week of school was exhausting. Tired of her own thoughts, she sat in the empty chair opposite a girl with a friendly face and deep dimples and nodded at her.

'I'm Empress,' she said to the girl. 'You okay?'

'I'm Emma.' The girl with the friendly face smiled.

'I'm Bridget,' another of Aniya's friends said. 'How's your second day going?'

'Is your name actually Empress?' *Another* friend of Aniya's asked, flipping her blonde hair over her shoulder.

Empress nodded. 'Yeah,' she said, putting a chip that had already gone cold into her mouth. 'What's yours?'

'Danielle,' the girl said, 'but everyone calls me Dani.'

'Mmm.' Empress put another chip in her mouth and chewed it slowly. 'And are either of those your real names?'

Dani jerked her head back. 'Yeah? What do you mean?'

'Nothing, don't worry.' Empress smiled.

'I was just *saying*, Empress sounds more like a nickname.' Dani shrugged.

'Well, it's not,' Empress just wanted to eat her food. 'I'd show you my passport as proof, but I don't have one.'

'Let's let her eat,' Aniya said finally. 'Anyway. Where are we all going on holiday this summer, girls?

'Nigeria with my family as usual.' A girl Empress had earlier understood was called Bolu said. Bolu was in the same maths class as her and Aniya, and seemed to be unbelievably good at fractions. Still not as good as Empress was, though.

'Really nice,' Bridget said. 'I think we'll be going to the south of France this year. Dad has bought a place there and has been renovating it for the last couple of months. Hopefully it'll be ready by summer break. You guys should def come out if you want.'

'I would, but I'll be in Jamaica and then Trinidad,' Emma shrugged. 'Obviously we usually do one or the other, but this year mummy wants us to do both. Should be fun though. My skin needs the sunshine.'

'We'll be in New York,' Dani smiled smugly. 'I love it so much there, it's basically, like, my second city. How about you, Empress?'

Empress almost choked on her chips.

'Me?' she asked.

Dani smiled and nodded. Empress wondered if Dani was trying to draw her out.

'I'll be in and around South London for my summer.' She smiled.

'Oh that's such a shame!' Bolu said. 'Why? Has something happened?'

'What do you mean 'why'?' Empress laughed. 'My family don't go on holiday.'

'Wait,' Dani cut in. 'When you said you didn't have a passport you weren't joking?'

Empress shook her head.

'So… you've never left England?' Emma asked.

'Nope.' Empress shook her head and pushed her tray away from her. The chips had gone too cold to eat by now and this line of questioning had taken her appetite away. She knew this would happen at this posh school. She knew that if she talked to anyone, they'd end up asking her questions about how poor she was. She just didn't realise it would happen this quickly. She thought she'd at least have a week to settle in before they realised she didn't belong at Chancellor School for Girls.

'Not even… for like a school trip or something?' Bridget checked.

'She said she hasn't been on holiday, girls! Just leave it,' Aniya said firmly. 'Anyway, Empress. You can come with me and my family this year, if you want! We're going to this cute little village in Italy. One of my dad's partners has a house there that doesn't ever get used, apparently.'

Empress smiled politely. She definitely was not going to a cute little village in Italy in the summer.

'What?' Dani asked. 'I usually come on holiday with you! How come suddenly your *assigned friend* is the one invited?'

'You'll be in New York,' Aniya reminded Dani. 'Besides, I'm trying to be nicer this year. My hormones and mood swings aren't going to take me over. Not anymore.'

'Hormones and mood swings?' Bridget snorted. 'I swear you've only said, like, three horrible things all your life.'

'Yeah, but even that's too much.' Aniya said. It was the horrible things in her head she was more worried about.

Chapter Two

Empress had been at Chancellor School for Girls for one week, and she was already exhausted. Not by the work, she could keep up with that no problem. That was why she'd been given a scholarship after all. Academics were no issue to her. She was easily the smartest girl in all of her classes.

She'd been trying to play it down because she didn't want too many eyes on her, but when her classmates would suggest that as a scholarship kid she wasn't as clever as they were, she had to show them that she knew more than them. It was all of *that* that was making her tired. All the social politics, all the having to prove herself. By the time she got home, all she could do was hang up her second-hand uniform, have a shower and go to sleep.

She hated the uniform, too. A shirt, a jumper, a skirt *and* a blazer that was made of the itchiest material she'd ever felt. And somehow, she could feel the itch of it through the jumper and the shirt. *Plus*, a tie that had to be a certain length. She'd had to stop off in McDonald's the morning of her first day to use the free WiFi so she could watch a tutorial on how to tie a tie.

'Hey!' Aniya smiled brightly as she took a seat next to Empress before their mid-morning Physics class started. 'How was Religious Studies?'

'Yeah, it was cool,' Empress shrugged. It was the only class they didn't have together, but she didn't really understand why Aniya would want to know how it was. She still didn't have Aniya figured out. Surely nobody was *this* nice.

'Oh, here you are!' Dani said, entering the classroom and spotting Empress and Aniya sitting together. 'The *assigned friends*.'

'Hey Dani!' Aniya waved.

'What's that smell?' Dani asked, taking a seat behind them.

Empress lowered her eyes. She knew it couldn't be her. Even if the hot water was off, she always found a way to bathe in the morning, even if it meant boiling the kettle a hundred times to fill the bath.

'Bridget!' Dani called across to Bridget when she came into class. 'Come sit next to me!'

Bridget picked up a textbook from the teacher's desk on her way to the desk next to Dani.

'Can *you* smell that, Bridget?' Dani asked.

'Smell what?'

'It's like… I don't know, I can't quite put my finger on it… it just smells like someone who hasn't washed.'

Bridget caught on to what Dani was doing, sniffing loudly.

'Yeah, I know what you mean.' Bridget leant forward so that she was right behind Empress, her nose practically touching Empress's braids. She took a big, loud sniff.

Empress's face felt as hot as lava. She opened her textbook and tried to concentrate on the words.

'I can't smell anything.' Aniya shook her head. 'Nothing at all.'

'Empress,' Dani began. 'Where did you get your blazer from?'

Empress ignored her.

'Hello?' Dani asked, leaning over her desk and tapping Empress on the shoulder.

'What?' Empress shot back without turning round.

'I said, where did you get your blazer from?'

'The same place you got yours, probably.' Empress said, eyes still on her textbook. Her eyes were blurring so much that she couldn't read any of the words.

'That's weird because... I didn't get my blazer from a homeless person.' Dani said.

'Dani!' Aniya hissed, turning around to face her friend. 'What are you doing?'

I'm just *joking*!' Dani said, holding her hands up. 'Don't overreact!'

'What do you mean you're joking?' Aniya stood up.

'Oh my *god,* Aniya, relax,' Bridget said. 'You know Dani's sense of humour.'

'Yeah, this isn't a sense of humour, this is just mean,' Aniya glared at Dani. 'Apologise.'

'Can you leave it?' Empress asked. 'I don't care what she said.'

'You see!' Dani said. 'Empress can take a joke.'

'Good morning, girls!' Mr Cooper, their English

teacher, walked into the room. His shirt was crumpled and the bags under his eyes looked even darker than usual. 'Aniya, why are you standing up?'

'No reason, sir.' Aniya sat down.

'Good!' He said, sitting down and looking at his pupils. 'Now, if you turn to page eighty, we can carry on where we left off last week.'

'Are you okay?' Aniya whispered to Empress.

Empress nodded and turned to page eighty.

'Ignore Dani,' Aniya whispered again. 'Okay?'

Empress ignored Aniya too.

Halfway through the lesson, Empress couldn't stop staring at the clock on the wall. It seemed to have stopped ticking and she couldn't wait for the bell to ring. Lunch was in half an hour and it couldn't come soon enough. She felt hungrier than usual today.

A few minutes later, she felt the stirrings in her stomach. Knowing what was coming next, she pushed a hand into her stomach, pressing it in so that it didn't rumble loudly.

It rumbled anyway. Aniya looked at it, shocked.

'Was that noise your stomach?' Aniya whispered to Empress.

Empress ignored her. But her stomach replied with a loud gurgle.

'I've noticed that you aren't eating,' Aniya whispered again.

'I do eat,' Empress whispered back, trying to concentrate on whatever thing Mr Cooper was telling them. Empress knew she knew more than him, but she didn't want to be called out for not paying attention.

Empress was always starving. Her growling stomach would usually wake her up at about three in the morning, so she'd shuffle out of her little boxroom and down the corridor to see if there was any food in the house (there wasn't usually anything apart from cereal or some of her little brother's baby rusks), then go back to sleep.

'Yeah, but chips doesn't count,' Aniya whispered *again*.

'Can we talk about this later?' Empress asked.

'Sorry, Empress and Aniya, am I interrupting you?' Mr Cooper asked.

'No sir,' Empress replied. She knew this would happen.

'Well, it seems like I am,' he said, folding his arms.

Empress knew what was coming next.

'Is it something you'd like to share with the class?' He pressed on.

Empress looked at Aniya, terrified that she'd tell everyone about what went (or, really, what didn't go) into her stomach.

'No,' Empress said. 'It's not.'

'I don't like your tone, Empress,' Mr Cooper said.

'Sir. I just said no. How else did you want me to say it?' Empress shot back. Her temper was something she was always working on.

'It was my fault, sir!' Aniya jumped in.

'Right,' Mr Cooper said, ignoring Aniya. 'Detention for you, Empress.'

'But sir, she didn't do anything!' Aniya exclaimed. 'Why are you giving her detention? Nobody ever gets detention here!'

'Do you want to join her, Aniya?' Mr Cooper asked. 'Because the way you're acting up, you can!'

'Fine!' Aniya said. 'This is unfair!'

'If you're going to disrupt my class then you can both get out.' Mr Cooper raised his voice to them, which made a few people in the class gasp.

This was the most drama anyone had ever seen in the history of Chancellor School for Girls.

'You serious, yeah?' Empress asked him.

'Very.' Mr Cooper exhaled loudly through his nose.

'Alright then,' Aniya said, packing up her things and throwing them into her bag. 'We'll go.'

Empress did the same. They stood up from their desk and walked towards the door. When they got there, Mr Cooper leaned towards Aniya.

'You know, Aniya, you need to watch who you hang around with. You have something close to a stunning reputation at this school, and don't forget it. Don't let yourself be dragged down.'

Aniya looked him dead in the eye. 'With respect, sir, it's not being dragged down when you're standing up for what's right.'

She looked at Dani and Bridget, so they knew that she hadn't forgotten their bad behaviour either.

'And at least my shirt is ironed,' she said to Mr Cooper, before she left the room.

'Let's go to the canteen,' Aniya said, walking ahead.

When they got there it was empty and quiet, while the dinner ladies got everything ready for lunchtime. Empress and Aniya sat down at a table by the big windows and let the shy spring sun stream in on them, while the clatter of industrial pots and pans played in the background.

'God, I've never been sent out of class before!' Aniya exclaimed, almost breathlessly.

Empress, who was no stranger to being sent out of class, laughed. 'You're less upset about it than I thought you'd be,' she said to Aniya.

'Why would I be upset?'

'Er, because as Mr Cooper said, you 'have a stunning reputation at this school'.' Empress imitated their English teacher so well that Aniya was shocked.

'Yeah, but I meant what I said.' Aniya shrugged. 'Detention for that? Ridiculous.'

'Won't your parents be pissed?'

Aniya shrugged again.

'Anyway, I haven't forgotten what we were talking about.' Aniya looked at Empress. 'What's going on with you and food? I've been watching since you got here and you literally… don't eat. To the point where I'm worried.'

Empress laughed again. 'What you worried for?'

'Empress, I wake up and have a massive breakfast, then I have a snack at eleven, then I eat a gigantic lunch, then I go home and have a huge dinner. And I'm still always starving. You, though? You eat *only* chips. And I can *always* hear your stomach rumbling.'

'Don't worry about me.' Empress rolled her eyes. 'I'm fine.'

'Okay, well, it's up to me if I want to worry about you or not.'

'But you don't know me,' Empress laughed.

'It doesn't matter. I can care about someone I don't know,' Aniya said, which Empress had to spend some time thinking about. She'd never heard that one before.

'Can I ask a question?' Aniya asked.

'...Yeah.' Empress replied tentatively.

'Do you have,' Aniya dropped her voice so that Empress had to squint and lean into her to hear the rest, '...an eating disorder?'

Empress shook her head.

'You can tell me,' Aniya said, putting a hand on Empress's. 'They're common, especially when

24

we're this age. Puberty and body image issues and all of that stuff because as soon as we have to buy a bra, society tells us we need to have the perfect body.'

'No,' Empress managed to say when Aniya took a small pause from talking. 'I just… I can't afford it.'

Aniya blinked a few times. 'What?'

'…I can't afford it.' Empress repeated.

'Afford what?'

'…food. Obviously?'

Aniya threw herself back in her chair. 'I didn't even… think about that, I am *so* sorry. Empress, I…' For the first time in maybe her entire life, Aniya was lost for words.

'But can we not make a thing about it please?' Empress asked. 'This scholarship doesn't cover food, which kinda make sense I guess, cos it's not like this is boarding school. And the food here is expensive! My mum doesn't have enough to give me big, big food money every day and do shopping for the house. And I've got a baby brother and he needs nappies and formula and all of that stuff, so. Costs money, innit.'

'But you do *eat* at home, right?' Aniya checked.

'Sometimes, sometimes!' Empress said. She didn't want to talk about this stuff, so tried to say as much as she could without making eye contact with Aniya. 'I guess I don't really think about it. If there's food there I eat it, if there isn't, I don't. I used to go to my nan's for dinner, but she died a couple years ago. And there's no other family cos mum cut them off. Anyway, I've got a neighbour who'll save me a plate every so often. It's cool.'

Empress finally looked at Aniya, who was on the verge of tears.

'Why you gonna cry, man? I don't want you to feel sorry for me, either!' Empress added. 'I'm fine! And I just know, yeah, that one day, I'll have a job that makes me so rich I can eat all the food I want, whenever I want. I'll even hire a cook.'

'Okay, great, and I'm glad you have that in mind,' Aniya said, throwing her head back so the tears didn't actually fall out. 'But we need to think about how you're going to eat properly *now*. Think about how smart you'd actually be if you weren't thinking about how hungry you were all the time. Or *even,* think about how much more you could focus when your body wasn't running on nothing.'

'I'm not taking money from you, Aniya,' Empress said. 'And I don't want you to buy me food, because your friends will see, and I don't want them to be telling people I'm so poor I can't eat properly. And I don't want to become your charity case. It's already bad enough that people know me as 'scholarship girl'.'

'Okay.' Aniya crossed her arms. 'Fine.'

'Thank you. Now can we stop talking about this?' Empress sighed.

'No, I'm not finished, I'm thinking still,' Aniya told her. '...Why don't you come to mine after school?'

'Er. Sure, I guess. Thanks.'

'No, I mean like, every evening,' Aniya said, very seriously.

Empress laughed at this. 'What?'

'No, hear me out,' Aniya began. 'You can come to mine after school, we can eat dinner and do our homework or whatever. So that way, you don't see it as like, a charity case thing. It's like, study group or something.'

'I don't know how I feel about this.' Empress narrowed her eyes at Aniya. 'Cos I feel like you feel sorry for me.'

'Get over that,' Aniya said. 'You're my friend, and I want good things for you. I'm sure you had friends in your old school who wanted to do good things for you, right?'

Empress didn't answer her.

'Right, so that's sorted.' Aniya smiled. 'We'll do detention or whatever, and then we'll go to mine.'

'Right.' Empress nodded, feeling a mixture of things she couldn't really pin down. She was suspicious, though. She was definitely suspicious.

Chapter Three

'How long 'til we get to yours?' Empress asked. They'd turned left off the street ages ago and had been walking on gravel for ages. There were so many trees around that she felt like she was walking through a park.

'Won't be long! The house is just past those trees over there. Dad wanted us as far from the road as possible,' Aniya told her. 'Because of his job, I guess. He's a barrister and I think he thinks he's got a lot of enemies. Even though I think it's just corporate stuff.'

They carried on walking. Empress decided it was just easier to listen to Aniya than to ask questions.

'Wait, wait. You live *here*?' Empress tried to stop her jaw from falling as she took in the size of Aniya's house when it finally revealed itself. It seemed to tower over her even though it was wider than it was high. Empress didn't even think it could be described as one house. It was like six houses all joined up, and with nothing but grass around it.

Empress had lived on an estate for as long as she could remember. She loved it, though. It was nice to have people around all the time. It made her feel less lonely, and everyone on the block knew her name. Most people were nice to her, too. On the flipside, she didn't know what it was like to wake up in the morning and not hear the sounds of her neighbours above, below and on either side of her waking up too.

They crunched up the gravel driveway, past two very shiny cars Empress knew were fancy but didn't know the names of.

'These are big cars,' she said to Aniya.

'Oh, yeah,' Aniya shrugged. 'Don't know why they're out of the garage. Dad must have just had them cleaned.

'So, you're *rich* rich.' Empress exhaled.

'I guess so,' Aniya said. 'But it is what it is. My parents work hard. Not that yours don't!' She added quickly. 'What… do your parents do again? Have I asked that?'

'Let's talk about that another time,' Empress said.

'I'm home!' Aniya shouted when they got into the house, her sweet voice echoing through the marble hallway. 'My friend Empress is with me!'

'Hello darling!' Empress heard a woman's voice call back from… somewhere in the house.

Empress literally could not believe where she was.

'Make yourself at home,' Aniya smiled, kicking her shoes off and putting a pair of fluffy slippers on. 'Hold on, let me get you some slippers.'

Aniya disappeared for a few seconds and when she came back, she was holding a box with the UGG logo on it. 'Here we go,' she said, opening the box and pulling out a fresh pair of black furry UGG slides.

'What?' Empress looked at Aniya blankly.

Aniya looked confused. 'What's wrong? Do you not like the colour? Sorry, these are the only spare ones we have.'

'No, no,' Empress said quickly. 'You just… have these in the house, new like that?'

'Yeah,' Aniya shrugged.

Empress noticed that Aniya always shrugged at things that were, in comparison, so hugely major to her.

'Put them on then!' Aniya said, putting the slippers on the floor in front of Empress.

Empress kicked her shoes off and slipped her feet into the slippers. They weren't actually as comfortable as she'd expected them to be, but she wasn't going to say that. Not that Aniya cared about her review, she was already off down a hallway.

'Come with me!' Aniya called back.

Empress followed Aniya's voice, and arrived in a huge, bright kitchen. Empress looked down at her slippers hitting the spotless tiled flooring as Aniya washed her hands.

'Right, let's make us a snack,' Aniya said, opening one of the slick grey cupboards. The whole kitchen could be described as slick, actually. It was all dark grey cabinets that you pressed to open instead of pulling the handles, and fancy electronics; Empress couldn't even guess what half of them were used for.

Empress washed and dried her hands. When she went to lean on the side, Aniya practically jumped on her head.

'Be careful!' Aniya shrieked. 'It's an Aga!'

'A who?' Empress asked, jumping away from whatever this thing that was apparently going to fight her was.

'An Aga,' Aniya repeated.

'You keep saying it, but that word doesn't mean anything to me,' Empress told her.

'Oh. Sorry.' Aniya rolled her eyes at herself. 'It's an oven. And these things are hot plates. So they're always on. I don't want you to burn your uniform.'

'Huh?'

'As in, these are hot plates. And they just stay on. So you don't have to preheat them. And they're good to keep the kitchen warm.'

'Is that very eco-friendly?' Empress asked.

Aniya ignored that and went back to the cupboard. She pulled out a bag of crisps, then went to the fridge, which Empress saw was stocked to the *brim*, and pulled out a pot of houmous.

'Have you ever had houmous before?' Aniya asked Empress. 'It's basically just blended chickpeas with–'

'I know what houmous is, Aniya.' Empress smiled. 'But it gives me belly ache.'

'Okay, well we have other dips,' Aniya said, inviting Empress to look in the fridge. 'Honestly, just help yourself.'

Empress stepped over to the fridge and spent a lot of time trying to take everything in. It was like every single posh food from them posh food shops like Waitrose had been put in there. Yeah, she might have known what houmous was, but there were loads of things in Aniya's fridge that she had no idea about. Some of the vegetables she saw looked *mad*. She'd ask about them another time, maybe.

'Honestly, I'm really fine, actually,' Empress said. 'I can just wait for dinner, you know. I'm good at telling myself not to be hungry.'

'No.' Aniya raised her eyebrows. 'You need to get better at saying what you actually want, Empress! You can't just go without because you don't want to bother anyone.'

Empress leaned on the non-oven bit of the kitchen counter and watched Aniya move about making her a sandwich. She wanted to say no, but she knew Aniya wasn't going to accept it.

'What do you want in here?' Aniya asked, holding up two pieces of bread.

'Er, I can't eat lactose. So, no butter, and no cheese or anything like that.'

'How about just peanut butter?' Aniya went over to the cupboard and pulled out a massive jar of the fancy-looking stuff.

'Yeah, that works, thanks,' Empress nodded. 'Thank you, Aniya. Really.'

'You don't need to thank me.' Aniya smiled, opening the jar.

'Right. Shall we go into the dining room?' Aniya asked when she was done, holding the plate for Empress in one hand and a bag of crisps in the other. 'Oh, you might want to grab a drink from the fridge. Or there's a water filter over there, glasses are in the cupboard above it.'

'I'm fine, I'm not thirsty,' Empress said. She *was* thirsty, but she was mainly overwhelmed.

'Oh my god, Empress.' Aniya put the plate and bag of crisps down, went over to the water filter and poured Empress a glass.

They made their way down a long corridor to the

dining room. It was huge, with a great wooden table and chairs in the middle that sat on wooden flooring, and paintings of parks and trees on the walls.

Empress shivered as she took it all in. Everything was as old and as fancy as it was in their school. The frames of the paintings were all painted gold. If that wasn't maximum posh then she didn't know what was.

'It is a bit cold in here, isn't it?' Aniya noticed. 'Even in the summer this room is cold. No idea why. I think I'm just used to it. Do you want a jumper?'

Empress knew why the room was cold – in all senses of the word. It was a massive space that was all wood and no personality. To her, it wasn't that different to their school gym.

'I'm good for a jumper, thanks. I'll be cool. Thanks for the sandwich,' Empress said, pulling out a chair, sitting down and taking a massive bite. It was heaven. She finished her mouthful before speaking. 'Didn't you want one?'

'No, crisps are fine for me.' Aniya put a Kettle Chip in her mouth and bit down. The crunch of it echoed around the room.

'Aniya?'

Empress sat up straight when she heard the voice of the woman before outside the dining room.

'We're in here, Mum!' Aniya called out.

'How was your day?' The woman asked before she entered the room. 'Oh, hello!'

A strikingly tall and beautiful dark-skinned woman with high cheekbones and pronounced lips walked into the room, her brown eyes narrowing in on Empress.

'Who have we here, then?'

'Mum, this is my friend Empress I was telling you about!' Aniya smiled. 'Empress, this is my mum, Dawn.'

'Hello,' Empress said quietly. She put her sandwich down because she felt like that was the polite thing to do.

'Ah, yes!' Dawn smiled. 'Empress who got the scholarship!'

Empress couldn't figure out if this was an insult or not. But she was in this woman's house, at her table, eating her food and drinking her fancy filtered water, so she wasn't going to argue with her.

'Yeah,' Empress nodded. 'That's me.'

'I didn't tell her about the scholarship,' Aniya

clarified. 'Mum is friends with our headmistress. As in, they talk all the time.'

'Well, it's nice to meet you, Empress,' Dawn said. 'I've heard good things. But, what I also heard was that the two of you were in detention.'

Empress's heart leapt into her throat.

'And did the school tell you *why* we were in detention?' Aniya asked her mum.

'They did.' Dawn nodded. 'And while I appreciate that you were sticking up for your new friend, and that, yes, you only thought you were fighting for what was "right", I also need you to remember that we pay a lot for your education. And with your exams coming up—'

'-Yeah, I know.' Aniya nodded, cutting her mum off. 'I know.'

'Yes, good that you know. But don't worry, I spoke to the headmistress–'

'Your best friend Beatrice, you mean?' Aniya cut in. 'You might as well just call her Beatrice, Mum.'

'—and it won't go on your record,' Dawn continued.

'Cool,' Aniya said.

'Cool?' Dawn raised her eyebrows at her

daughter.

'Cool,' Aniya repeated.

'Anyway, we'll talk about this more at dinner,' Dawn said, pursing her lips. 'Your father will be in at about seven, so we'll eat at seven thirty. And less snacking before then, please.'

Dawn left the room, disappearing back down the dark corridor she came from.

'Are you... sure I should stay for dinner?' Empress checked with Aniya. 'Your mum seems pissed.'

'She's always a bit like that. She's just not that warm.'

Just like the house, Empress thought.

* * * *

After they did their Physics homework, which didn't take long because Physics was genuinely Empress's best and favourite subject, it was time for dinner. As they cleared their stuff from the table, an older white woman with dyed red hair sort of popped out from nowhere and started putting dishes of hot food on the table.

'Empress, this is Emily.' Aniya introduced

the woman, who Empress guessed was the housekeeper or something. Or maybe the cook, who knew? These people were so rich that they probably had staff all through the house.

Empress waved at Emily, who returned a big friendly smile at her. 'I hope you're hungry, Empress!' Emily said. 'And what a beautiful name!'

'Thank you!' Empress smiled. 'Do you want help with anything?'

'Oh no!' Emily laughed as she shuffled back to the kitchen. 'Please, don't trouble yourself!'

'It all smells *divine*!'

Empress looked up at the man whose voice had boomed into the room.

'Hi, Dad!' Aniya smiled at her dad as he walked into the dining room and sat at the head of the table. He was a tall, handsome man who looked a bit like a budget Obama.

Empress could see that Aniya had her mum's rich skin tone, but her dad's soft features.

'Dad, this is Empress, my friend from school. Empress, this is my dad. But you can call him Abib.'

'Empress!' Abib smiled widely, as he rolled the sleeves of his shirt up. 'That's a case of nominative determinism if I ever heard one. Your mother must be a very smart woman.'

'A case of… huh?' Empress asked. She was smart, but this was a bit far.

'Nominative determinism,' Abib repeated. 'It's a hypothesis, not sure where it comes from actually. Anyway, it's a hypothesis that people end up growing into their names. So, in your case, your mother obviously expects you to grow into royalty in some way. Unless you are already royalty, in which case I beg your pardon.'

Empress laughed. How was Abib so fun and his wife so cold?

'Nah, I'm not royalty,' Empress told him. 'I don't even know why my mum chose it, actually.'

'Hello, darling.' Dawn entered the room again. She walked over to her husband and kissed him on the cheek. 'How was your day?'

'It was the same as it always is, really.' Abib smiled. 'But how nice to come home and meet a new friend of Aniya's! And we were just talking about her name.'

'Oh, really?' Dawn asked as she walked to the other end of the table and sat opposite her husband. 'What were you saying?'

'Well, we were talking about the meanings of names, and before you came in and distracted me with your beauty, my love, I was *actually* about to say that many, many years ago, I was in Oman for work, and I met this wonderful young woman named Aniya. And she was so kind to me that I always thought about her—'

'Careful, darling.' Dawn smiled at her husband as Emily entered the room and started serving the food.

'No, not like *that*, not like that. Anyway, I remember looking the name up a few years later, and it means 'loving' in Arabic. Isn't that nice? So, when Aniya came along, I thought it would suit her. And it does! So, I guess another case of nominative determinism, isn't it, girls?'

'I knew about the loving part,' Dawn said. 'You never told me about your *friend* in Oman.'

'Anyway, let's move on from all of that, shall we?' Abib picked up his fork and started eating.

'Um, what… is this please?' Empress asked quietly. 'There are a couple things I'm allergic to, so…'

'Oh god, of course!' Abib exclaimed. 'I should have checked! If I'm not mistaken, it's polenta, and a mushroom ragout. Are you okay with those things?'

'I'm okay with mushrooms.' Empress nodded. 'But what's... polenta?'

'Polenta is ground corn,' Dawn explained.

'Ah!' Abib began. 'Where are your family from?'

'Jamaica,' Empress told him.

'Ah, the same as Dawn's family.' Abib smiled. 'And have you ever had cornmeal porridge?'

'Yeah, my nan made it all the time.' Empress nodded.

'Well, it's the same thing. Polenta and cornmeal. Just different names.' Abib smiled. 'So you'll be fine. I promise.'

When they were finishing dessert, Abib asked Empress if she'd told her mum where she was. She told him that her mum probably wouldn't notice that she wasn't home.

'My mum doesn't think about what I'm up to very much,' Empress told him. 'I don't think she even remembers my birthday.'

'If her memory is that bad, how on Earth did she fill in your scholarship forms?' Dawn, as sharp as a knife, quizzed her.

'I did my own scholarship forms.' Empress

shrugged. 'I filled them in, just got her to sign them.'

'What made you think to do that?' Dawn asked.

'I hated my old school. I didn't learn anything, really. Just ended up teaching myself. And I walked past Chancellor one day and wondered if it would be better. So, I went on the website and yeah. Just… did the rest.'

'God,' Dawn sighed. 'That sounds like the plot of a rags-to-riches movie.'

'Well, *we'll* remember your birthday,' Abib said, wishing his wife could be a little bit *nicer* to this poor girl who was sat at their table. 'When is it?'

'Sixteenth of March,' Empress said.

'Seriously?' Aniya asked, leaning across the table so quickly that she almost knocked her glass over.

'Yeah?' Empress looked confused. 'Seriously.'

'That's the same as me!' Aniya exclaimed.

'Ah!' Empress smiled. 'Twins, yeah?'

'Maybe that's why we're such good friends!' Aniya said. Empress couldn't believe how excited she was.

'Maybe!' Empress said, a little bit too flatly for Aniya's liking.

'Anyway, what with detention, and now this revelation, that's a lot of excitement for one day.' Dawn pushed her chair back and rose from the table. 'Abib, would you mind driving Empress home?'

Empress felt a horrible knot form in her stomach.

'I'm fine, it's just one bus home!' she told Dawn and Abib, panic in her voice.

'Don't be silly,' Abib said. 'We're not having you going home alone in the dark!'

'Honestly, it's fine. It's still a bit light out.' Empress really did not want these people seeing where she lived. *She* didn't mind where she lived, but she didn't want to be judged by these posh people. 'I've been getting around by myself much later than this for a long time, trust me.'

'Mmm and that's not a good thing, Empress,' Abib said. 'Let your food digest before you get your stuff together, then come and find me.'

The second Abib left the table, Emily came to clear the dessert bowls and glasses away.

Aniya, now convinced that because she and Empress shared the same birthday they had a psychic link, got up from her seat and walked around the table so that she was sitting next to Empress.

'Sorry if this has all been overwhelming for you,' she said, 'I'm so used to it that I forget that all this can be a lot.'

Empress wanted to cry. She couldn't put her finger on why.

'And honestly,' Aniya began. 'I don't care where you live. My dad doesn't care where you live. I'm not going to suddenly not want to be your friend because of your house. And if you want, we can just take you to your road or something. And you can text me when you get inside.'

'Yes, please,' Empress nodded. 'Thanks, Aniya. For a lot.'

'That's what friends are for, Empress,' Aniya smiled.

Chapter Four

'Sooo, your birthday is coming up!' Dani said to Aniya, bouncing the ball over to her.

'Yes!' Aniya said, catching it and twirling it over in her hands. 'And Empress's!'

'We know,' Bridget sighed, adjusting her netball bib.

'What are we doing for it?' Emma asked. 'Remember last year when your parents hired us a limo and we drove around town? Why don't we do something like *that* again?'

'Mmm, no.' Aniya threw the ball over to Emma. 'That was a bit much. I'm thinking that we could do a sleepover at mine, maybe?'

'A sleepover?' Dani snorted. 'You're turning

sixteen, not eleven, Aniya.'

'Yeah, but I want to do something for both me *and* Empress. Like, she doesn't go in for all that showy stuff.'

'Only because she can't afford it,' Bolu said. 'I'm sure she'd be grateful for a taste of the high life.'

'Don't be mean, Bolu!' Aniya stared daggers at her friend. 'We don't talk about people like that.'

Bolu rolled her eyes and caught the ball that Emma threw at her.

'Whatever,' she said, throwing the ball towards the hoop. It bounced off the rim and hit Dani on the shoulder.

'Ow, Bolu!' Dani pouted, rubbing her shoulder.

'It didn't hurt that much,' Bolu said. 'And it was an accident.'

'Anyway,' Aniya continued, picking up the ball as it rolled towards her, 'I'm thinking a sleepover with lots of food and films. It'll be nice. Come if you want, don't if you don't.'

She positioned herself in front of the hoop, bent at the knee and released the ball as she came up. The ball swished straight through the hoop.

'Um, Aniya,' Dani began, still rubbing her shoulder even though everyone knew it definitely didn't hurt anymore. 'Are we going to talk about the fact that we never see you anymore?'

'What?' Aniya asked. 'You're literally seeing me right now.'

'Yeah, only because Empress is in hockey and not basketball,' Emma said.

'Are you being serious?' Aniya laughed.

'Yes!' Bolu said. 'Very serious!'

'Guys, I like all of you just as much as I like Empress. She's new and I was her assigned friend, what did you want me to do? Desert her?'

'No,' Dani started, 'but you and her are basically joined at the hip. You spend *all* your time with her. And we were here first!'

'Yeah. She was your assigned friend and she's become, like, your *best* friend,' Bridget added. 'She goes to your house every day after school *even though* you spend all of your time with her, and all of *our* time with her *at* school.'

The words of her friends stung. Yeah, she thought she was doing a good deed at the beginning by making sure Empress ate and stuff, but Empress was actually a really nice person to be around.

There was something about Empress that she

really loved. Empress was different to all of her friends, who had, if she was honest with herself, started to annoy her more since Empress arrived. She realised how yappy her friends were. All they spoke about was who was the most popular and who had the most TikTok followers. Empress didn't even *have* TikTok. She didn't even have data most of the time.

And Empress saw the world in a different way. She hadn't been sheltered in the way Aniya or her friends had. She actually understood stuff about real life, even if she could be a bit down about things. But actually, Aniya even liked that about Empress. She wasn't the sort of person who would put a front on that everything was fine, and that the world was fine. Empress had made Aniya realise that the world was only fine if you had money.

'I love you all,' Aniya finally said, catching the ball as Bolu threw it to her. 'Equally. You're all my best friends.'

Aniya didn't *really* mean this. She'd noticed the way they'd been treating Empress. At first, she thought it was jealousy, but she began to realise that it ran deeper than that. They were just...

mean girls. Empress's arrival had made her see who they really were.

'So, why is it she's at your house every day then?' Bridget asked. 'You both just go straight off and none of us are invited.'

Aniya felt bad. 'I just— I wanted to help her,' she said quickly.

'Help her how?' Dani asked.

'Basically, I noticed that she wasn't eating,' Aniya began. 'Well, she would just always have chips, and I thought it was weird. And I asked what she eats at home and she said that she basically doesn't eat. So I thought, maybe if she comes to mine after school, she can eat something proper. And it's been really nice, and my parents love her. Well, my mum took a bit of time because my mum doesn't love anyone, really, but my dad loves her. And if you guys actually spoke to her about anything other than *"what it's like living on an estate"* you'd see why she's so great.'

Aniya finished speaking and finally took a breath.

'Wait,' Emma laughed. 'You're basically being like, her personal Marcus Rashford?'

'Don't say that,' Aniya said, instantly realising the mistake she'd made. She shouldn't have told them.

'I can't believe this!' Dani exclaimed. 'Feeding Britain's children, one scholarship case at a time!'

'Can you not say anything, please?' Aniya pleaded with her friends. 'She'll hate that I've told you.'

'There's not really anything to tell,' Bolu said. 'We all knew that she was poor. We saw it when she walked in with her second-hand uniform.'

'Third-hand by the looks of things.' Dani laughed. 'Have you not seen where she's clearly had to stitch that blazer pocket back on?'

'Girls, I want to see that ball moving!' Miss Marks, their PE teacher, shouted across the playground at them.

Before she knew what she was doing, Aniya twisted the ball in her hands and pushed it away from her chest with force, directly into Dani's face.

Dani's scream cut through the playground, and everyone turned to look at her. Blood was pouring from her nose.

It was only when she saw the blood dripping on to Dani's netball bib that Aniya realised what she'd done.

'Oh my god... I am... so sorry,' she whispered, backing away as the rest of her friends huddled around Dani.

'Right, I don't know or care what's gone on,' Miss Marks said as she ran over, 'but I saw what happened, so you're going to need to go and get changed and head *straight* to the headmistress.'

Aniya stood there, opening and closing her mouth. She didn't know what to say.

'Speechless, Aniya?' Miss Marks said, parting the girls. 'Me too. Go. Now.'

Aniya walked towards the changing rooms, bursting into tears as she heard Miss Marks say, 'I think it's broken.'

* * * *

That evening, Aniya lay in her bed feeling both angry with herself, and sorry for herself.

'Aniya!' She heard her mum call her from the stairs. She decided to be asleep.

'I know you aren't asleep,' Dawn shouted up. 'I heard you moving a few seconds ago.'

'What is it?' Aniya called back.

'You know what it is,' Dawn shouted. 'Can you come down and talk to me and your dad, please?'

Aniya dragged herself out of bed to go and face the music. When she got downstairs, she could hear her parents talking in the reception room.

'Yeah?' she said to them.

'Shall we try that again?' Dawn asked.

'Yes Mum, yes Dad?' Aniya said.

'Sit down, Aniya,' Abib said gently.

Aniya crossed the room and sat on the sofa in front of them.

'I know what you're going to say,' Aniya began. 'And I'm sorry, because it was kind of an accident and not. Because you know Dani is my friend, but the stuff her and the other girls have been saying to Empress has been so horrible, and at first, I was kind of like, oh they're joking, but then it started to get really horrible. Like, all this stuff about her name was kind of silly, and then they said some stuff about her hair which I was a bit like, hmmm, about. But then they said some stuff about her smelling, even though she doesn't smell! And then in maths, when Empress knocked her calculator on the floor and it broke, Bridget said 'it's a shame you can't afford a new one', and—'

'–Right.' Dawn held up her hand to stop Aniya from speaking so much without taking a breath that she'd faint. 'Remember what you need to do when you get like this?'

Aniya breathed in, taking the air right down to the bottom of her stomach.

'Well, the good news is that you aren't being suspended, though it was close. I can't keep getting your headmistress to do me favours.'

'Well, maybe it would do me good if you just let me get punished properly,' Aniya shrugged.

'Not with the record that you've got,' Dawn said. 'It's practically perfect, and we want to keep it that way.'

'My love,' Abib began. 'We know you've been having some troubles with your feelings. But you know you can talk to us about it, don't you? It's no use bottling it all up and then exploding when it gets too much for you.'

'I know, but it's hard to even talk about it because I don't know what it is!' Aniya told her parents. 'Sometimes, most of the time, I'm fine, and then suddenly, bam, I want to cry, or shout, or something, I don't even know!'

'But where does it come from, my love?' Abib asked Aniya, going to sit next to her on the sofa.

'I don't know.' Aniya started crying and Abib immediately put his arm around her. 'It must be hormones or puberty taking a long time to settle or something. Because I don't really have anything to cry about. It's not like we don't have a nice house, or I don't go to a good school.'

'Well, it doesn't matter how much you have,' Dawn said. 'You're allowed to feel things. I certainly do. And your father does.'

'Your mother *certainly* does,' Abib said. 'I'll never forget, when she was around your age, she got into a fight with one of her best friends for something similar. I was the one to have to pull her away from the fight! I've never been so scared of someone in all my life!'

'Really?' Aniya sniffed, wiping tears from her face.

'Oh, absolutely.' Dawn nodded. 'Being fifteen is hard, for so many reasons. You're not a child anymore, but people start treating you like you know more than you do because you're a bit taller and have some more sense about you.'

'But you're still a baby,' Abib said gently.

'I'm not a baby!' Aniya sniff-laughed.

'Well, you're our baby.' Abib smiled.

'And you can talk to us,' Dawn said. 'About anything. You mustn't push it down.'

* * * *

A few days after *the incident*, the Friday before Aniya and Empress's birthday, the two girls were leaving the canteen when Dani appeared in front of them. Her eyes were bruised and on her nose was a gauze pad.

'Hey, Dani,' Aniya smiled. 'How are you doing?'

'You can *see* how I'm doing,' Dani said, pointing at the gauze pad on her face.

'I'm sorry,' Aniya said. 'You know I'm sorry. I was angry and I shouldn't have done it. I don't know what else I can say to you.'

'Have you told your new best friend why you did this?' Dani asked her, then looked straight at Empress.

'How am I involved, please?' Empress asked. 'I don't wanna be involved in any of this. I wasn't even there.'

'Please, just leave it,' Aniya pleaded, grabbing Dani's arm gently.

'Well,' Dani smirked, shaking Aniya's hand off her. 'I maybe made a *little* insensitive joke– and it was a *joke* – about you. But *only* because she told us you were her charity case and she had to feed you or whatever.'

'Are you serious?!' Empress exploded.

'Empress, I'm sorry!' Aniya turned to her best friend, who had already stormed off.

'Why would you do that?' Aniya shouted at Dani. 'What's *wrong* with you?'

'What's wrong with *me*?' Dani spluttered. 'You broke my *nose*, Aniya! What's it going to look like when it's healed?'

Aniya chased after Empress, who was heading to the science block.

'Empress!' she called after her.

'I don't wanna chat to you!' Empress called back as she sped up. She ran into the empty Physics lab, slammed the door behind her, and then threw herself on to one of the stools.

Aniya went in and sat down opposite her. She didn't say anything for a while. She just let Empress do her heavy breathing. She decided that she'd let Empress speak when she was ready.

After five minutes of panicking that Empress would never say anything to her again, Aniya thought she was going to explode. She had so many things that she wanted to say, and it was almost killing her to hold it in.

When Empress finally opened her mouth to speak, Aniya closed her eyes, wincing as she waited for Empress to drag her, but after a few seconds she heard sniffling. She opened her eyes and saw Empress crying.

'Oh my god!' Aniya jumped up, ran around the desk and wrapped her arms around Empress's shaking shoulders. 'Empress, I'm so sorry!'

'Why did you tell them that?' Empress asked Aniya between sobs. 'I asked you not to tell them! It's already bad enough here without all of that shit.'

'I know, and I'm sorry!' Aniya said, hugging Empress tighter. 'They were getting on at me about you always being at my house, and I think I felt like I should explain, and as soon as I said it, I realised I shouldn't because clearly I can't trust them. But it's not their fault. I'm the one who messed up.'

Empress exhaled slowly.

'You're squeezing me really tight you know,' she said to Aniya.

'Sorry!' Aniya said, springing off Empress. 'Wait, let me get you a tissue.'

Aniya went into her bag and pulled out a packet of tissues. She handed them to Empress, who took one and blew her nose very loudly.

'Thanks for apologising,' Empress said, throwing the soggy tissue in the bin. 'I forgive you. It's fine.'

'What?' Aniya couldn't believe it.

'What d'you mean *what*?' Empress looked confused.

'No, as in, you can be annoyed at me if you want,' Aniya said. 'For as long as you need to be.'

'But you've apologised,' Empress said. 'People don't apologise to me very often. Or ever, really. It means a lot.'

Aniya felt like her heart was going to break. She wished she could go back in time and give Empress a nicer life.

'Bell's gonna go soon,' Empress said, blowing her nose on a fresh tissue. 'What food we having tonight?'

'You're still coming?' Aniya squealed.

'Of course,' Empress nodded. 'Why would I miss our birthday sleepover? This is like, the first time anyone has done anything for my birthday.'

* * * *

'How's your vegan pizza?' Aniya asked Empress.

'If I'd known vegan pizza would be normal pizza without cheese, I would have suggested we get something else,' Empress said flatly.

'Is it that bad?'

'It is what it is.' Empress shrugged. 'Do you want to try it?'

'No, thank you.' Aniya shook her head.

'Thought you'd say that.'

'Empress?'

'Mmm?'

'How do you feel about spells?' Aniya asked, skimming her laptop with one hand and putting a slice of pizza in her mouth with the other.

'Huh. What do you mean *spells*?' Empress asked from the other end of the bed.

'Like, witchy spells,' Aniya said.

'Yeah, I'm not into all of that,' Empress laughed. 'Good for you if that's what you're on though.'

'No, I'm not *into* spells, someone just posted this and I thought it might be fun.' Aniya swung the laptop round so that Empress could see what was on the screen.

'A spell to see through the eyes of someone else?' Empress read slowly. 'I thought you was gonna show me a love spell or something so you could finally get the guy who works in that café down the road to talk to you.'

'No!' Aniya laughed. 'I don't have time for boys right now.'

'But you have time to see through the eyes of someone else?' Empress checked. 'Right.'

'Why not?' Aniya smiled. 'We're basically in each other's heads anyway. It'll be fun! If it works, I think you'll literally be able to see yourself sitting opposite me and vice versa.'

'Why would I wanna see myself sitting opposite myself?' Empress groaned. 'I know what I look like, Aniya. I could just go and look in the mirror.'

'Come on, let's do it.' Aniya jumped up. 'Come on, come on!'

'Alright man, fine.' Empress laughed.

'Okay, so it says we should sit opposite each other.' Aniya read out loud. 'So, you just come a bit closer.'

Empress climbed across the bed and got closer to Aniya. She crossed her legs and faced her. 'Alright, done.'

'Wait, hold on, I'm going to get a candle.' Aniya jumped up like she'd realised she left her straighteners plugged in hours ago.

'Why do we need a candle?' Empress sighed. 'It's already enough and a lot that you're making me do juj and now you're making it more weird than it already is.'

Ignoring her friend, Aniya rummaged in her desk drawer. 'Nothing here,' she said, folding her arms and putting on her thinking face.

'Why are you doing your thinking face?' Empress asked. 'Come on, man.'

'One sec.' Aniya ran out of the room. A few minutes later, she came back in, holding one of her mum's very expensive scented candles in one hand and a packet of matches in the other.

Empress threw herself back on the bed.

'Right, I think now we're ready' Aniya said, climbing on the bed. She lit the candle and balanced it between them.

'So you want to set us on fire?' Empress asked, putting the candle on the bedside table. 'Smells nice though.'

'Great. Glad you like it.' Aniya skimmed the laptop screen. 'Now it's saying we need to read this spell at the same time.'

'Do we really need to do it at the same time?' Empress sighed.

'Yes!' Aniya told her. 'Come on. Wait, I think it's Latin. We have to repeat this phrase three times.'

Empress looked back at Aniya blankly.

'Okay, let's both close our eyes and take a deep breath.'

Empress did as Aniya told her. She didn't have it in her to argue.

'Now open your eyes and let's read it at the same time. Three times, remember?'

Empress opened her eyes and nodded. They both looked at the screen and said, three times in unison:

'ab uno disce omnes, ad oculos. ab uno disce omne, ad oculos. ab uno disce omnes, ad oculos.'

'Now let's close our eyes, and when we open them, we should be able to see ourselves from the other's eyes,' Aniya commanded.

'Yes, you said.' Empress closed her eyes.

'Okay, let's open them on three, two, one—'

They opened their eyes slowly. 'What can you see?' Aniya asked Empress.

'Oh my god, this is so weird,' Empress said.

'What, what, what, what can you see?' Aniya

gasped, grabbing Empress's hands.

'I can see… my very, very gullible friend sitting opposite me,' Empress laughed.

Aniya looked disappointed.

'Happy birthday, though!' Empress smiled.

'Already?' Aniya asked.

'Yeah, it turned midnight like, thirty seconds ago.'

'Happy birthday!' Aniya jumped on Empress and hugged her. 'Do you mind if we do presents in the morning? I've got one for you. And I know my parents got us something, too. And usually we all open them together.'

'Sure.' Empress nodded.

They got ready for bed. Just before Empress fell asleep, she rolled over and asked Aniya a question. 'What did it translate to? The spell. Like, what does it mean?'

'Something like: 'from one, learn all, with your own eyes'.'

'Oh, okay. Cool.' Empress said. 'Night. Happy birthday.'

'Night.' Aniya whispered. 'Happy birthday. And by the way—

'Mmm?'

'I'm really glad we're friends,' Aniya said. 'I

think being around you makes me calmer. I'm not sure why.'

Empress didn't say anything.

'Just wanted you to know.' Aniya said, looking over at her friend. Empress was already dead to the world.

Aniya smiled and turned the lamp off.

Chapter Five

When Aniya woke up, she felt out of sorts. She blamed it on the pizza and rolled out of bed to go and get some water. She didn't want to open the curtains and disturb Empress, so bumped into everything on the way to the door. When she got to the kitchen, she saw her mum making her morning cup of coffee.

'Happy birthday! And good morning,' Dawn said. 'Did you sleep well?

'Yes, thanks.'

'Is my birthday girl up yet?' Dawn asked.

Aniya smiled. It was nice that her mum was properly embracing Empress into the family.

'She's still asleep,' Aniya said.

'Okay. Well, when she's up, both of you come down and we can do presents,' Dawn said, making her way out of the kitchen. 'If there's anything you can't find, just shout.'

Aniya blinked slowly. 'What?' she asked, but her mum had already left the kitchen.

Bleary eyed, Aniya got some water before going back upstairs. She threw herself back into bed, downed the contents of the glass and dozed off.

* * * *

'ANIYA!'

Aniya woke up with a start when she saw herself standing over... herself. 'It did the thing! The thing did the thing! The thing! The eyes thing!' She heard her own voice babbling.

Aniya jumped up, ran over to the mirror and looked at herself in the late morning sun that streamed through the curtains. Longer arms, longer legs, and a whole different face, obviously. She was... Empress.

Empress, in Aniya's body, was pacing up and down the room behind her.

'Didn't you say you found this spell on the

internet?' Empress shouted. 'Who posted it?'

Aniya closed her eyes and opened them again. This was all a dream, she thought. It was all a dream, she was going to wake up soon, and she and Empress would go downstairs and have a nice birthday breakfast.

'Aniya, why are you closing your eyes?' Empress squeaked. 'This isn't going to go away!'

Aniya opened her eyes and looked into her own panicked eyes.

'Okay, let's calm down,' Aniya said, getting back into bed. 'Let's just try and be logical about this.'

'Logical?' Empress asked. 'I'm literally standing here in front of you in your body, Aniya. How we gonna be logical?'

'It's going to be fine,' Aniya said, to herself more than to Empress. 'We're going to flip it. Or, best case scenario, it'll wear off after a day or something.'

'Wear off after a day or something?' Empress repeated deliriously. 'Where are these instructions you're reading? Where did you find this spell? Let me see what the page says.'

Aniya opened her laptop and found the page. Empress sat down next to her and they read it at the same time.

'It doesn't say there's a way to reverse it.' Empress said. 'So, we're stuck like this forever?'

'Calm down, calm down.' Aniya put a hand on Empress's shoulder.

'God, I've got soft skin haven't I?' Aniya said, stroking the body Empress was in.

Empress looked at her blankly. 'Is now the time for vanity?'

'It's not vanity,' Aniya said. 'It's a very strict body skincare routine that I've been doing for months. I just didn't know it was paying off.'

'Fine, whatever,' Empress said. 'But what are your parents gonna say when we go down and tell them what's happened?'

'We're not telling them!' Aniya exclaimed. 'They wouldn't believe us anyway. Even *I* don't believe this!'

'So, what do we do?' Empress asked, her breathing speeding up.

'Okay, so, first of all, take a deep breath,' Aniya instructed. 'Here's what we do. We shower, we get dressed, we go downstairs, and we act as normal as possible. Then, we get in contact with the person who posted the spell in the first place, and we reverse it.'

'How can you be so *calm*?' Empress wailed.

'Because what else is there to do?' Aniya asked. 'I'll shower first. And I'm sorry but… I'm going to have to see you naked. Obviously.'

'This is the worst day of my life,' Empress groaned.

'Okay! Rude!' Aniya said. 'What are you trying to say about my body?'

'When you shower, keep your eyes closed tight,' Empress told Aniya. 'And I'll do the same.'

'Okay, okay, relax. Where are your clothes?' Aniya asked.

'In that bag.' Empress pointed at her battered rucksack in the corner of the room.

'Okay, cool.' Aniya nodded. 'And I'll leave you some of my clothes to wear outside the bathroom.'

'Thanks.'

'Have a nice shower!' Aniya smiled, looking at herself. Looking at her own body like this was maybe the first time she didn't see the things she'd spend so much time being insecure about.

'Are you being sarcastic?' Empress asked her.

'No!' Aniya said. 'Go shower! We have a birthday breakfast to get through.'

The girls showered as quickly as possible. Taking a shower was actually incredibly hard when your eyes are closed the whole time, it turned out. Especially for Empress, who had no idea where anything was or what any of the knobs did. When she went back into the bedroom, dressed and shivering, Aniya looked up and asked her why her teeth were chattering.

'I didn't know how to turn the water up and didn't want to open my eyes to look!' Empress told her.

'Jesus Christ, Empress.' Aniya rolled her eyes. 'You can look if it means you don't give my body a cold. When I get back in there, I want to find it how I left it.'

'I'm not going to give your body a cold!' Empress said. 'Trust me, nobody wants to give your body back how you left it more than me.'

'Okay,' Aniya said, standing up and smoothing Empress's tracksuit down. 'Ready for breakfast?'

'I guess I have to be, innit?' Empress shrugged, catching herself in the mirror and pulling Aniya's clothes down. These little dresses Aniya wore weren't very comfortable.

'Good morning my birthday girls!' Abib beamed when Empress and Aniya entered the dining room. 'How are we feeling on this fine Saturday? Are we feeling sixteen?'

Both girls laughed awkwardly as he pulled them into a big hug. They didn't know how to answer the question at all.

'Sit down, sit down!' Abib smiled. 'Shall we eat and then presents? I know Emily has made a very special breakfast for the occasion!'

Emily entered and put a bowl of something Empress *did not* understand on the table next to a spread of scrambled eggs, croissants and various jams, crumpets, toast and smoked salmon.

'Happy birthday, girls!' Emily looked at Empress and Aniya and smiled. 'God, Aniya, it feels like only yesterday I started working here. You know, you were five when I first met you. And now look. Sixteen!'

Dawn walked into the dining room, presents in hand. She put them down on the table and walked over to who she thought was her daughter and planted a quick kiss on her forehead. 'Happy birthday, my darling,' she said, wiping her lipstick off of Aniya-but-Empress's head.

'Thanks… Mum,' Empress said.

'Tuck in, don't let it get cold!' Abib said, gesturing at all of the food on the table. 'And Aniya, Emily made your favourite!'

Empress looked over at Aniya nervously, trying to communicate with her eyes that she had no idea what 'her favourite' was.

'Caviar!' Aniya said, pushing the bowl over to Empress. 'You told me this was your favourite when we first met, didn't you?'

Empress widened Aniya's eyes. 'You know what? I think I've gone off it, you know.'

'Really?' Dawn asked. 'But Emily went and got it especially! Just have a little bit, darling.'

Dawn spooned some of the caviar on to a piece of toast and handed it over to who she thought was Aniya. 'Don't make a fuss.'

'You know, I've forgotten exactly what caviar is,' Empress said, taking it and looking down at the small black bubbles.

'What? Really?' Abib asked. 'Is this what's happening at the ripe old age of sixteen? You're losing your memory already? It's fish eggs, Aniya.'

'Right. Yeah. Okay.' Empress started to feel sick at the thought of them. 'Sorry, I really don't think

I can try— have it. I feel a bit weird. The pizza from last night, I think. I might just have some dry toast.'

'Oh no!' Abib said sympathetically. 'Not food poisoning on your sixteenth birthday! What a total disaster!'

'I did *tell* you not to order from that place,' Dawn reminded her before taking a sip of her coffee. 'But as usual, nobody listens to Mum.'

'Sixteen-year-olds aren't really meant to listen to their mums, Dawn,' Abib said to his wife. 'Don't take it so personally.'

On the other side of the table, Aniya was eating everything. She was starving. She had no idea how Empress could bear being this hungry all the time. She pushed her third croissant into her mouth and washed it down with a big gulp of tea. She followed that with a buttery crumpet, then, she started to cover her toast in butter. Every single corner was dripping. So much so that when she pushed it into her mouth, butter dripped down her chin. She wiped it away with the back of her hand happily.

'An— Empress?' Empress said to her friend. 'You've taken your lactose intolerance pills, right?'

'My wha...?' Aniya had completely forgotten that Empress was allergic to milk. At that second, the cramps kicked in, deep in her stomach. 'Let me go and get them! They're in my bag, right?'

'Yeah.' Empress said pointedly. 'I think I saw them in there this morning.'

Aniya practically flew up the stairs and into the bathroom.

For a while, Empress picked at her breakfast, listening to Aniya's parents speaking about the extension on the house they were planning. She didn't say anything for fear of giving herself away. Even if she wanted to join in with the conversation, she couldn't. They were talking about all of these grand design plans that were going over her head.

'Is Empress okay?' Abib eventually asked Empress, concern across his face.

'Yeah, she'll be fine,' Empress said. 'It won't last long. She just needs to get it all out.'

'Darling!' Dawn was horrified. 'We're at the dining table!'

'Sorry,' Empress said, embarrassed. 'I... forgot.'

'It's fine,' Dawn said. 'But don't forget where you

are next week. I don't want you saying something to put them off.'

'...what's happening next week?' She asked Aniya's mum. 'Who is *them*?'

'You've got your interview with your father's firm to do their summer internship, Aniya!' Dawn told her. 'You can't tell me you've forgotten about that!'

'Sorry, no, I didn't forget!' Empress said. Aniya hadn't told her about this.

'Well, I hope not,' Dawn said. 'That internship is just the beginning! It's the perfect start to your journey to follow in your father's footsteps.'

'It's all set out for you.' Abib smiled. 'You don't have anything to worry about. You're going to be an even better barrister than me. I can tell.'

Empress felt anxious at the thought of *anyone's* life being set out for them at sixteen. She started to feel panic rise in her chest.

'I'm just going to go and check on An— on Empress,' Empress said, excusing herself from the table.

When Aniya was finally finished on the toilet, she held on to the sink to steady herself. It had been a horrible half an hour. She heard a gentle knock on the door.

'I'm just coming,' she whispered, hoping it was Empress outside.

Aniya left the bathroom, closing the door behind her quickly. 'I wouldn't go in there if I were you.'

'You're meant to be taking care of my body!' Empress hissed. 'This is *much* worse than giving your body a cold. Look how bloated my stomach is!'

'I'm sorry, I forgot!' Aniya said. 'It's fine though, I feel much better now.'

'Oh, good,' Empress said sarcastically.

'Do you actually have lactose intolerance pills, though?' Aniya checked. 'I could definitely do with a couple.'

'No!' Empress said. 'They're expensive, Aniya. Which is why I avoid eating every buttery thing under the sun!'

'Okay, I get it!' Aniya said. 'Do you *think* you will cheer up if we do presents?'

Empress rolled Aniya's eyes at her. 'Yes,' she said, turning and heading back down the stairs.

'Everything okay, Empress?' Abib asked when the girls went back into the dining room.

'Yeah,' both girls said at the same time.

Aniya shot a look at the real Empress.

'I was also saying that Empress is fine,' Empress said from Aniya's body. 'Because yes, she is fine now.'

'Did you have your pills?' Abib asked.

'I did, but I think my pizza was funny, too,' Aniya said, rubbing Empress's bloated stomach.

'Oh, my love!' Abib said sympathetically. 'Can I get you anything? Maybe some ginger in hot water? That should settle it.'

'I'm fine thanks Da— Abib. Sorry! Almost called you Dad there.' Aniya laughed. 'Sorry, it's just... you're like a Dad to me, I guess.'

Empress wanted to bang her head on the table. How could Aniya be in her body and be embarrassing her so much?

'You girls are being very peculiar this morning,' Dawn assessed. 'You must have stayed up too late.'

'Shall we do presents?' Empress suggested. She needed to get Aniya out of this house as soon as *possible*. Nobody would be at her home to clock how weird she was being anyway.

* * * *

After the girls managed to hold present giving down, Empress practically pulled Aniya out of the house. They said they were going out for the day, and that they were going to stay at Empress's that night for a change of scenery.

Dawn resisted, obviously, but Abib said it would be good for Aniya to see how the other half lived.

'Fine, but no more pizza,' Dawn told them. 'And Aniya, call us if anything comes up.'

They got the bus to the library, riding it in near silence.

'Are you annoyed with me?' Aniya asked Empress.

'Obviously,' Empress shot back.

'Even though I got you such a nice present?'

'It's a nice present, yeah, but there's no point me having a chain with an "E" on it if you're gonna be the one wearing it.' Empress looked out the window.

'It's going to be fine, Empress,' Aniya said.

Empress turned and looked dead into her own eyes, which she'd been avoiding. Even though it wasn't really *her* in her own body, her eyes still looked sad.

'Do you promise?' she asked Aniya.

'I do,' Aniya told her, taking her friend's hand. 'Seriously, I can't believe how *soft* my hands are.'

'Shut up, Aniya!' Empress laughed.

Chapter Six

'Okay,' Aniya said when they arrived at Lewisham Library. 'There should be *some* book in here on reversing spells.'

'In Lewisham Library?' Empress asked flatly. 'A book on reversing spells?'

'Well, we might as well check.' Aniya sighed. 'What do *you* suggest? I don't know where the nearest witch shop is!'

As they got to the doors, a group of boys around their age who were lurking outside stared at them.

'What?' Empress asked the boys. 'Can we help you?'

'Nah,' the shortest boy said, stepping towards them. 'But I can help *you*.'

'I don't think you can help me with anything.'
Empress rolled her eyes.

'That little dress you're wearing can help *me*
though,' the boy said, licking his lips.

'How can you wear a dress like that and think
we ain't gonna look?' Another boy said, a smirk
playing across his face.

'Um, excuse me" Aniya said. 'But the way that *I*
dress doesn't invite eyes *or* commentary.'

'The way you dre—?' the first boy said. 'We're
talking to your friend. *Not* you.'

'The way *I* dress doesn't invite *eyes* or
commentary,' the second boy mocked Aniya.
'Nobody was talking to you, *tracksuit*. You sound
like a teacher.'

'Oh my god, it's not even worth explaining
a woman's worth to you,' Aniya said, pulling
Empress into the library as the boys burst into
loud adolescent laughter.

'Hello!' Aniya practically jumped over the front
counter. 'Do you have any books on spells?'

'Aniya, man,' Empress hissed.

'What?' Aniya swiped Empress away.

The plump, grey-haired woman who was

arranging some books behind the counter pulled her glasses from where they were resting on her head down to her eyes.

'Books on what, sorry?' she asked, squinting at the two girls in front of her. The one in the tracksuit, who she recognised, looked unusually happy. The other one couldn't stop pulling her dress down.

'Any books on spells?' Aniya repeated, smiling so much that Empress could see all of her own teeth for the first time in her life. Aniya was such a smiley person, she thought. Then she tried to remember the last time she'd ever had a reason to smile that wide. She couldn't think of one.

The woman sat down and started tapping on the computer. 'Okay so we've got *The Spells Bible: The Definitive Guide to Charms and Enchantments* by Ann-Marie Gallagher, or we've got *Curses* by Nicola Morgan,' she said after a minute or so.

'That's lucky,' Empress said sarcastically.

'Perfect!' Aniya beamed. 'Where are they please?'

The woman tapped away again.

'Oh, I spoke too soon,' she said, looking up at the girls. 'They've both been taken out.'

'By *who*?' Empress asked. 'How many people are doing up spells?'

'*But* there's a copy of *The Spells Bible* at East Ham CSC library, and a copy of *Curses* at Acton Library, if you don't mind the journey,' the woman told them. 'Do you want me to write that down for you?'

'Yes, please!' Aniya trilled, as Empress rolled her eyes and leaned back on the counter.

'Thank you!' Aniya smiled again, reaching for the piece of paper that would hopefully hold the key to all of their problems. She folded it up and put it in the pocket of Empress's tracksuit.

'God, these things are comfortable, aren't they?' she said, pulling the hood up so that it covered her head completely.

'Why do you think I wear them?' Empress shrugged.

They left the library and walked past the boys again, who stayed quiet until the girls were a few feet away. As soon as they were far away enough, they started shouting various things about what they wanted to do to Aniya's legs.

Empress, who had been catcalled a *lot*, whether she was wearing a skirt, leggings or a floor-length puffa jacket, turned on her heel and charged back towards them. Even if it wasn't her body they were talking about, she wasn't going to let them think it was okay.

'Listen,' she said, pointing a finger at them. 'I was polite at first and I was gonna leave it, but you've carried on being pricks.'

'What you gonna do?' The main boy laughed. 'You gonna get your friend to lend me her tracksuit?'

'What? That's not even funny.' Empress narrowed her eyes at him, at the same time resisting the urge to pull Aniya's dress down. She could tell that it had ridden up. 'But I'm gonna walk away again, and if you say one more word, or if I hear one laugh or snigger, I'm gonna come back, and even though I'm wearing a little dress, I'm gonna rock your jaw so hard all your boys are gonna have to take you Lewisham hospital.'

The boy rolled his eyes. Even though this girl looked cute, it looked like she was going to follow through with her fighting talk.

'Whatever,' he said, turning away from her.

Empress walked a few steps away from him, then turned back. The boys were looking at the floor.

'That's what I thought!' she called back, as she joined Aniya.

'Er, what would have happened if one of those boys had hit you?' Aniya asked. 'Don't forget that's my body you're in.'

'They weren't gonna do anything. Boys like that just talk, talk, talk to impress each other,' Empress said. 'And I know it's *your* body I'm in. It's your body I was defending.'

'Hmmm.' Aniya crossed her arms.

'Hmmm what?' Empress asked.

'Before we go to East Ham or Acton or whichever mission we're about to go on, can we get some food?' Empress asked Aniya.

'Yeah, but…' Aniya began.

'But what?'

'My stomach isn't feeling too good, you know. I need the bathroom. I think it's still recovering from the dairy.' Aniya rubbed Empress's stomach. 'I don't know how you do this.'

'Well, I *don't* do this.' Empress rolled her eyes. 'I don't think we should go back to the library to use the toilet because I don't wanna get into it with those boys again, but we'll find somewhere.'

'Oh,' Aniya said. 'I can't use public toilets.'

'Huh?'

'I can't use them.'

'No, I heard what you said,' Empress said. 'But I just... why?'

'Because they're toilets for the public,' Aniya said. 'And I know that sounds awful and you're going to call me posh or whatever, and I know the privilege in saying this, but even the thought of using them makes me feel stressed.'

'I—' Empress began. 'Do you know what? I'm not even gonna say anything.'

'Can we just go to yours?' Aniya asked. 'It's not far from here.'

'What choice do I have, Aniya?' Empress asked through gritted teeth. 'What choice do I have?'

* * * *

'Well. Here's the block.' Empress gestured to a high-rise building sitting in the middle of an estate that was so tall it seemed to kiss the sky. It was surrounded by concrete buildings like it, but none were as high. There wasn't a tree in sight.

'It's nice!' Aniya said a bit too quickly for Empress's liking.

'You don't need to lie,' Empress said. 'You could just say nothing.'

'Hey, don't be like that with me,' Aniya said. 'You know me enough by now to know that I don't say things I don't mean!'

Empress nodded. Aniya was right.

'Sorry,' Empress said. 'I just feel a bit... you know. Anyway.'

'I know,' Aniya said.

'Right. So, when we go through, people are gonna be saying hello. I know you like to chat, but nobody knows me as chatty like that, so I'm gonna need you to keep it moving. You just say hi and you keep walking. You don't need to introduce me – or you – you know what I mean.'

Aniya listened carefully to the instructions, nodding as she took them in.

'Okay, but what if someone really needs to talk to you?' Aniya asked.

'They won't,' Empress said.

'But what if they do?' Aniya checked.

'What does anyone *need* to talk to a sixteen-year-old girl about?' Empress folded her arms and blinked slowly at Aniya.

'Well, what if they want to say happy birthday?'

'Aniya.' Empress bent over and exhaled slowly. 'Please.'

Trying to rein Aniya-as-Empress in was like a military operation, it turned out. Whenever *anyone* they'd walked past said hello, Aniya would say hi back and ask how their day was. She offered to help people with their shopping. She helped one woman on the ground floor hang her washing. She even tried to give directions to someone lost on the estate, even though she had *no* idea where she was sending them.

'You're a liability you know,' Empress said, when they finally made it into the lift. 'You're too nice for your own good.'

'Is that a bad thing?' Aniya said.

'Er, *yeah*,' Empress said as she pressed button thirteen and the lift rumbled to life. 'Thank god it's working today.'

'But isn't it nice to be nice?' Aniya asked.

'Remember my first day of school? And you told Miss Tribble that you didn't want to look after me or whatever?' Empress recalled. 'That's the energy you should keep round here.'

'Yeah,' Aniya said. 'But I don't want to be like that. And I'd been having a bit of a weird time. Which comes and goes. But. It's definitely better now. I hope.'

Empress didn't say anything.

'Did it upset you?' Aniya asked her.

'What?'

'When I said I didn't want to look after you.'

'Nope.' Empress shook her head. 'I'm used to that.'

The lift pinged, opening on the thirteenth floor. They left the lift and entered a dank corridor. The lights were flickering and buzzing like a hundred moths were trapped in the large industrial bulbs.

'Careful where you step,' Empress said, walking ahead. 'Wait, can you hear that?'

'Hear what?' Aniya asked.

'Crying,' Empress said, speeding up. They reached a red front door that had clearly had graffiti washed off it more than once. By the keyhole there was splintered wood where the door had been kicked in and repaired, kicked in and repaired.

The crying was louder. 'Where's the keys, Aniya, where's the keys?' Empress was panicking. Aniya had never heard her own voice that panicked before. 'Hand me my rucksack!'

Aniya threw Empress's rucksack off her back and over to her and Empress reached into the front pocket. She pulled the keys out and opened the front door, running into the flat.

Aniya stepped in behind her and had to take a few seconds to let her eyes adjust to the mess. She'd never seen anything like it. There was rubbish everywhere. It filled the hallway. Half of the wallpaper had been ripped off the walls, and there was writing over the top. Scrawled words Aniya couldn't quite make out that had been written in biro.

Aniya followed the sound of the crying into a living room that was even dirtier than the hallway. She saw Empress in the middle of the room rocking a weeping baby boy gently. Aniya got closer and saw that he was wearing a stained red t-shirt. His nappy looked and smelt very full.

'Aniya, would you mind looking to see if there are any nappies around?' Empress asked. 'I just need to calm Leo down.'

'Where's your... mum?' Aniya asked, fixed to her spot.

'Your guess is as good as mine.' Empress shrugged as she bounced Leo up and down in her arms. 'A nappy, please? I need to change him.'

'Okay.' Aniya nodded. 'Where will it be?'

'Again, your guess is as good as mine. Just have a look around, please.'

Aniya left the living room and kicked through the rubbish on the floor into the kitchen. She looked through all of the cupboards. No nappies and no food.

She went into the room next to the kitchen. All that was in there was a mattress on the floor and a chest of drawers. She could tell that it was Empress's room from the edge control and toothbrush on the windowsill.

Still, no nappies. She left Empress's room and went back down the hallway, opening the door to a small bathroom. It had no windows, so Aniya pulled the cord to turn the light on. Nothing happened. She took her phone out of her pocket and turned the flashlight on. She scanned the room with the light. The toilet was stained dark brown, and the bath was thick with dirt and grime. On the side next to the leaking sink were two fresh nappies. Aniya grabbed both and ran with them into the living room.

'Here we go!' Aniya said, trying to sound positive and upbeat. Which was quite hard to do in Empress's voice.

'Thanks.' Empress took the nappies, cleared a space on the floor and lay a changing mat down. She placed Leo on it gently. While Empress got to changing his nappy using the last of a packet of wipes she'd found amongst the mess, Aniya crossed the room and went over to the balcony door.

'Can I open it?' she asked Empress.

'Yeah.' Empress nodded. 'Sorry about the smell.'

'No, it's not that!' Aniya said.

She opened up the balcony door and stepped out. She'd never been so high up in her life. She thought she was going to have a nosebleed.

'You can see, like, all of London from here,' Aniya said to herself. She couldn't believe her eyes.

'WHO ARE YOU?' Aniya heard a voice shout from the living room. She ran back into the room and saw a plump Black woman with unkempt hair standing in the doorway. She had dried spit round her mouth and her eyes were wide, blinking rapidly. She was looking down at what, to her, was Aniya, a stranger, changing her baby.

'I'm Aniya,' Empress said. 'A friend of your daughter's.'

'A friend of my daughter's?' The woman shrieked. 'What are you doing here?'

'Mum, Mum,' Aniya said, running over to the woman. 'This is my friend Aniya from school.'

'And why is she in my house?'

'I'm in your house because me and Empress needed to get something quickly, Pauline,' Empress said, finishing up with Leo and picking him up off the floor.

'Pauline?' Empress's mum laughed. 'And you're calling me Pauline? Yuh *bright*.'

'Why was Leo alone?' Empress asked Pauline.

'Oh! So you've brought this little girl into my house to play social services?' Pauline shouted at Aniya.

Aniya blinked back at Empress's mum. Anger rose up in her. 'Well, Mum,' she began, 'if you could look after me and Leo properly then you wouldn't have to worry about anyone coming in here, would you?'

Pauline threw her head back and laughed. Empress looked at Aniya and shook her head. 'Please,' she mouthed at her friend.

Aniya ignored her. 'What's wrong with you?' she shouted at Pauline.

'That's strike two,' Pauline said, itching her head roughly. Aniya watched dried flakes fall across Pauline's shoulders.

'How can you leave Leo by himself? He's a tiny baby! Anything could have happened!' Aniya shouted.

'Right,' Pauline said. She ran over to who she thought was Empress and grabbed her by her long extensions. She dragged her into the kitchen by her hair and pushed her up against the counter.

Before Empress could run in and stop Pauline, Pauline closed the kitchen door in her face and jammed a chair under the handle to stop her from coming in.

'That'll stop your little friend from coming in,' Pauline spat, moving closer to Aniya. 'Ever since the day I had you, you were a nuisance.'

Aniya leaned back, away from Pauline.

'Just like your dad. Too smart, smarter than anyone else. And you let everyone know it as well.

Nobody told you to go off to that fancy school and now look, you're bringing people to this house too. You know I don't like people in our business!'

Empress was afraid of what Pauline could be saying to Aniya. She put Leo down in the living room and ran into the hallway. She tried to open the kitchen door, but the handle wouldn't go down.

'You're a bad girl, Empress,' Pauline continued, hearing the door handle rattle against the chair. 'Always been bad. Rotten. I can't wait until you leave this house. Ever since you were born, and your father left me with you, I can't wait until you get out. He should have taken you with him. But instead, he left you here as a reminder of him. Every time I look at your face it's his I see.'

Aniya tried to slow her breathing down as she listened to what Pauline was saying. She tried to put herself in Pauline's shoes to understand how someone could spout these words of hate and pain to her own child.

'I'm sorry you feel that way.' Aniya said, pushing Pauline away from her. Pauline stumbled back and narrowed her eyes suspiciously at who she thought was her daughter.

Aniya walked over to the door and kicked the chair away from it. As she went to open it, Pauline pushed past her and into the hallway.

'You're different.' Pauline pointed a finger at who she thought was her daughter before turning and opening the front door.

She stepped through it and slammed the door behind her, the impact of which cracked the frosted glass pane that sat above the door number. Baby Leo started crying immediately.

'What did she say in there?' Empress asked Aniya.

'Nothing of any truth,' Aniya said. 'Don't even think about it.'

Empress started to cry. Leo was so shocked he stopped his own crying. 'I'm so embarrassed,' she sniffed.

'Don't be,' Aniya said, hugging her. 'Will she come back?'

'Yeah, but probably not 'til tomorrow,' Empress told her. 'This is her way.'

'Okay.' Aniya understood. 'I'll stay here with you and Leo tonight.'

'Yeah, but there's not a proper bed, or hot water, and the electric has gone, and—'

'We'll figure it out!' Aniya said, cheerfully. 'But maybe we should go out and get something to eat. Just to have a bit of... space from this place, you know? Get some air. Change of scenery.'

'Okay, I get it.' Empress nodded.

* * * *

Aniya held the door of the café open, so that Empress could push baby Leo's pram through the door, and the man behind the counter immediately had his eyes on them.

'You!' He called across the café before the door even closed behind them. 'Take your hood down if you're coming in here.'

Not realising he was talking to her, Aniya ignored him and walked up to the counter. Empress stood back next to the pram and laughed to herself.

'Hood!' The man repeated when Aniya was closer. 'Off!'

Aniya blinked back at him.

'What?' she asked.

'This is three times I've said now. Hood off.' The man's voice was getting louder.

'Oh!' Aniya said, reaching up to the hood when she realised it was on. 'Why?'

'Because I said so!' the man said.

'But I don't understand what rules and regulations you have in place that mean I can't wear a hood to eat,' she put to him.

'Hoods mean trouble,' the man shouted.

'Are you serious?' Aniya laughed.

'I am serious!' the man shouted again. 'You come in here with your friend and her baby and wearing a hood! And so young! It's trouble!'

'I beg your *pardon*?' Aniya crossed her arms. '*Not* that it's got anything to do with you, but that baby is my friend's little brother! And we happen to go to Chancellor School for Girls! So, this *trouble* that you're referring to isn't going to come! And even if that *was* my friend's baby, and we didn't go to school at all, that *still* doesn't give you the *right* to *discriminate* against us!'

The man behind the counter was confused by the words that were coming out of this hooded girl's mouth. The people eating their evening meals had stopped to watch the commotion and were looking at him, tutting and shaking their heads with disappointment.

'I don't care what you say!' he shouted; his pride bigger than his ego. 'Get out!'

'My dad is a barrister,' Aniya said to him before she turned to go. 'You haven't seen the last of me.'

'You're not really getting your dad involved, are you?' Empress checked with Aniya as they walked out.

'No.' Aniya shook her head. 'He told me he'll only step in when it comes to the big things.'

'What are the big things?' Empress asked, swerving the pram to avoid a pile of dog poo on the ground.

'I haven't found out yet,' Aniya said.

'Look, I know you think we should get air or whatever, but I'm tired, Leo is tired. You're probably tired.' Empress sighed. 'Today has been a lot.'

It was true. Aniya had never seen her own eyes so tired.

'Let's go back to yours.' Aniya nodded. 'We'll go on our mission for *The Spells Bible* tomorrow.'

* * * *

Later that night, they lay on Empress's mattress, a thin sheet covering them all. Baby Leo gurgled between them as he fell asleep.

'What time is it?' Empress asked.

'It's only ten,' Aniya said, looking at the time on her phone. 'It feels like it's been the longest day in history.'

'Night, Aniya.' Empress said. 'And… I'm sorry for my mum. She wasn't always like that, you know. I think having Leo sent her over the edge a bit. Well, over the edge a lot.'

'Don't apologise,' Aniya said, 'You don't need to say sorry for her. Or what she does. I'm just glad I could see what's been going on, I guess.'

'What did you say the translation of that spell was again?' Empress asked.

'From one, learn all, with your own eyes.' Aniya said, word perfect.

'Well, you got what you wished for.' Empress laughed before closing her eyes. 'You've seen it all.'

'And what have *you* seen?' Aniya whispered to Empress.

'I've seen that you know right from wrong, and you'll always fight for it. But I clocked that quite early,' Empress said. 'I guess from today, I know that you're loyal. Very loyal. You've seen my life and you don't judge me for it. And I get it. Your life seems kind of perfect from the outside. But I also get that people – well, your parents, I guess – kind of make you feel like you have to be perfect. I feel trapped being you, I guess.'

'Yeah, but it feels... maybe ungrateful, to say that,' Aniya said. 'But yeah. I think that's where a lot of my weird anger comes from. I feel like I'm expected to be *good*.'

'You are good,' Empress said sleepily.

A few minutes passed.

'And I'd never judge you,' Aniya whispered. 'I think you're the most amazing person I've met.'

Aniya looked over at Empress, whose eyes were closed. She was fast asleep.

* * * *

The next day, Aniya woke up before Empress did. She looked at baby Leo who was still sleeping peacefully, then lay on her back for a bit thinking about how she really wanted a croissant. 'Wait,' she said out loud, then looked down at her hands.

'Empress!' Aniya whispered. 'Empress!'

'What, what is it?' Empress groaned, rolling over to face her.

'I'm me!' Aniya said, a little bit louder. 'I'm me! Are you you?'

'Shit,' Empress said, sitting up and looking down at her arms and legs. 'It reversed!'

They both stood up and squealed, holding on to each other and jumping up and down on the mattress, away from baby Leo who could clearly not be woken up by anything.

They left him asleep in Empress's room and started to try and clean up the house. 'We're going to need some black bags,' Empress said. 'Shall we go shop?'

'Yeah, we should get some food as well.' Aniya nodded.

'It's always about the food with you, innit?' Empress laughed.

'Yes, it is!' Aniya said. 'And now I know what it's like in your body, I can't believe you aren't all about the food too!'

Empress rolled her eyes.

'And please, let me pay for the stuff,' Aniya added. 'We've gone through enough for you to be arguing with me over ten pounds in the shop.'

The girls bundled Leo into his pram and set out to the little Nisa Local on the edge of the estate, keeping an eye out for Pauline. They didn't see her on the way there, or on the way back. Which was a relief, but also worrying.

Once they'd fed Leo, then themselves, they tidied the flat as much as they could.

'You should go home,' Empress said, knotting one of the black bags closed. 'Not that I want you to. More like, if I know my mum, she's going to come back soon, and it'll be better for both of us if you aren't here.'

'I'm not leaving you here to deal with *that* woman by yourself!' Aniya protested.

'*Trust* me, Aniya,' Empress sighed, 'please. We'll be fine. She just needs to come in and shout at me a bit more and then she'll end up talking to herself and falling asleep like usual. It'll be fine.'

'You're always saying it's fine when it's not!' Aniya's voice shook.

'Okay,' Empress said. 'Well. It is what it is, then.'

Aniya's head was overflowing with thoughts all the way home. She'd decided to walk to celebrate getting her body back, but was so troubled by what had gone on that she could barely put one foot in front of the other.

When she finally made it back, she entered the house quietly, ran upstairs and had a shower.

When she was done, she stood in front of the mirror in her bedroom and rehearsed what she was going to say a couple of times.

'Mum. Dad.' Aniya walked into the kitchen and looked at her parents. The people who had raised her, who had looked after her, who had always protected her from harm, and had done it all with kindness, even though her mum could be a bit harsh with it sometimes.

'Can I ask you something?'

'You can ask us anything, darling,' Abib told his daughter as he pulled a plump grape from the bunch in the fruit bowl and popped it into his mouth.

'Mmm, of course,' Dawn added, placing a bit of cheese on a cracker.

'I know this is a big question. And you're

probably going to want to say no. But can you please promise me that you'll at least hear me out?'

'Of course, my love.' Abib smiled gently.

'Aniya, what is it?' Dawn asked, putting the cheese and cracker down. 'You're scaring me.'

'It's not scary,' Aniya told her mum.

'Let her get it out in her own time.' Abib reached across the kitchen table and took his wife's hand.

'Okay, so,' Aniya began, 'you know I went to stay at Empress's?'

'Oh god, what happened?' Dawn lurched forwards in her seat.

'Nothing mum, relax!' Aniya said. 'Nothing like that, nothing bad. I'm obviously fine.'

'I knew I shouldn't have let you go an—'

'Dawn,' Abib said firmly. 'Let Aniya speak.'

'Mum, Dad. When I met Empress, I knew she was living in a bad way. But I didn't know how bad, I don't think. Probably because you two have made sure I haven't had to live like that, and that I haven't even needed to see people living like that. Thanks for that, I guess. But, yeah. Empress is living in a really bad way.'

Aniya took the time to explain, in as much detail as possible, what had happened when she'd gone to stay at Empress's. She tried not to cry because she knew it wouldn't really help but broke down when she explained how Empress's mum spoke to her. 'And I don't want her to be there anymore. I don't think it's safe for her because like, there's no food, and no water, really, but most of all, I don't think it's safe for her head. I don't know how she's survived up until now.' Aniya looked up at her parents.

'Okay,' Abib said. 'Your mum and I need to talk about this. Can we have Empress's mum's number?'

'I don't have it.' Aniya shook her head. 'I don't know if she even has a phone.'

'And where is Empress now?' Dawn asked

'She's still there with her little brother,' Aniya told her parents.

'Right.' Abib smiled gently at his daughter. 'Me and your mum are going to have a talk, and then we'll come and find you. Okay? Why don't you go and have a little rest?'

Aniya nodded and stood up. She left the room and closed the door gently behind her. Instead of going to have a little rest like her dad suggested, she stood by the kitchen door and put her ear close to the wood so she could hear every word. She'd been doing this since she was a child and they hadn't caught her once.

'Are you surprised?' Aniya heard Dawn ask Abib.

'I'm not,' he said. 'Not at all. But even so, you know.'

Aniya heard Abib let out a deep sigh.

'We have to do something,' Abib said.

'Of course we do,' Dawn agreed. 'Do we tell the authorities? No, I don't think we do. I don't want that poor girl in any system.'

'No, no, god knows what foster care would do to her,' Abib said.

'Well, I think it's obvious what we do, isn't it?' Dawn asked her husband. They both knew the answer.

* * * *

An hour later, Abib was knocking on Pauline's door, Aniya standing behind him. Pauline answered, baby Leo hanging off her hip.

'Can I help?' she asked, looking Abib up and down.

'Hello, my name is Abib.' He introduced himself at the same time Pauline spotted Aniya behind him.

'Oh, it's *you*,' she said in *the* direction of Aniya. 'EMPRESS, WHAT TROUBLE YOU BRINGING TO MY DOOR? AGAIN.' Pauline bellowed down the hallway.

'No, no trouble,' Abib said. 'May we come *in*, please?'

Pauline squinted her eyes at him before stepping into the hallway and heading towards the living room.

Abib and Aniya followed her in. As Abib walked through the hallway, he couldn't believe what he was seeing. It was worse than how his daughter had described it.

'Is it okay to sit down?' Abib asked even though he didn't really want to sit down. He could see mouse droppings covering the sofa.

'Do what you want,' Pauline said, putting baby Leo on the floor. 'Now, sir, can I help you?'

'Right,' Abib started, quite nervously, even though he was used to fighting cases in the High

Court. 'So, you've met my daughter Aniya. She's good friends with your daughter, Empress.'

'I knew that little bitch had done something!' Pauline spat. 'That girl always ruins everything. EMPRESS, COME HERE. *NOW*!'

'No, no, I've said before, Empress has done absolutely nothing wrong—'

'–Why you so posh?' Pauline cut Abib off. 'You police?'

'No, not police, I'm a barrister,' Abib told her.

'Mmm.' Pauline snorted.

'Anyway, as I say, Empress hasn't done anything wrong. In fact, it's really the opposite. From what I understand, she's an exemplary pupil, she's fulfilling all of the requirements of her scholarship, exceeding them even, and—'

'Cut to the chase. I don't have the time for all this big chat and these big words.' Pauline waved her hand in Abib's direction. 'Wind it up.'

'Well. In the simplest terms, me and my wife have discussed it, and we believe that it would be safer, and better, for Empress to come and stay with us. For as long as needs be.'

'What?' Pauline scowled at Abib. '*My* Empress?'

'Yes,' Abib said, sitting up straight.

'You think I'm going to go and let my daughter live with two people I don't know?' Pauline laughed. 'You must have another thing coming.'

Aniya saw a crack of light from Empress's room shine into the hallway. She squinted and saw Empress's shadow in the light. Her right leg was shaking the way it always did when she was anxious.

'Okay. Well. Let me give you some options,' Abib said in a voice that Aniya recognised was his fighting voice. 'Either I call social services first thing tomorrow morning; and I should let you know that I am very, very close friends with the Head of Social Services in this borough. I call them in the morning and let them know exactly how Leo and Empress are, in effect, neglected, here with you. They'll be taken from you and put in the system. Or, if Empress is happy to, you let her come with us tonight, and on Monday, my wife and I start the process of legally adopting her. We would offer to take Leo too, but Empress is already part of the family, and we think that it might be better for a baby to be with his mother, if you can get yourself straight.'

Pauline laughed again, but this time, she sounded afraid.

'It's up to you, Pauline,' Abib said firmly. 'But I think you know that you need to do what's best for your daughter and your son. And I assure you, she will be safe with us. You can of course have our address, and we can set up visits, through the proper channels, obviously. We aren't taking Empress away from you, but we need for her to be safe.'

'And what happens when she's eighteen? When she's an adult?' Pauline asked. 'What then?'

'Well, if all goes to plan, she'll be in our care until she doesn't want or need to be anymore. But we certainly aren't going to push her out the door when she turns eighteen. We'll treat her like we treat Aniya.'

Pauline narrowed her eyes at Abib.

'Empress!' She bellowed. 'HOW MANY TIMES HAVE I CALLED YOU?'

Aniya watched Empress come into the hallway and walk shakily, into the living room. 'Yes, Mum?'

'You want to go with these people?'

Empress didn't answer.

'Empress?' Pauline hissed at her daughter.

'Speak up, nuh?'

Empress nodded, tears falling down her face.

'I said *speak*,' Pauline shouted.

'Shouting at her isn't going to do anything,' Abib stood up and growled at Pauline. Aniya looked up at her dad, surprised. She'd never heard this tone before.

'Yeah,' Empress said quietly, 'I do.'

'Well you better pack up your tings and go,' Pauline said, going to pick baby Leo up from the floor.

'Mum, I—' Empress tried to find some words, maybe an apology.

'I don't need to hear it,' Pauline sneered.

'I'll leave my details for you.' Abib took his notebook and a pen out of his jacket pocket and started to write his full name, number and address on one of the pages.

'Don't bother.' Pauline pushed past him, Leo in her arms. 'She's your business now. Let yourselves out.'

And with that, Pauline slammed out of the front door. They watched her outline disappear through the cracked frosted-glass pane in the door.

'And how do you feel that went?' Abib checked with Empress and Aniya.

'I just want to get out of here,' Empress whispered.

'Okay.' Abib nodded. 'Aniya, do you want to go and help Empress pack up her things?'

The girls went upstairs and, an hour later, they were sitting in the back of Abib's car. The boot was full of black bags of Empress's clothes, books, make up – everything a sixteen-year-old could have, which was, in this case, both a little and a lot.

Aniya turned to look at Empress. The bright lights from the cars coming towards them illuminated Empress's face, which was wet with tears.

Aniya put a hand on Empress's, and Empress held it tight.

'I don't even care about her,' Empress said quietly. 'But I didn't even get to say goodbye to Leo. That's my baby bro, man.'

Empress burst into loud, heavy sobs.

'It's okay, Empress,' Abib said from the front of the car. 'We'll be home soon.'

They pulled up to the house. Dawn was already on the front steps waiting for them.

Empress stepped out of the car and went to open the boot.

'No, no, we'll deal with all of that tomorrow.' Abib said gently, putting a hand on Empress's shoulder. 'You go inside.'

Empress walked towards Dawn. 'Thank you, Dawn. I don't know how to thank you, though. Maybe I could do some work around the house, or get a job, or—'

'You don't need to thank me, you poor girl.' Dawn pulled Empress into her arms. 'You're just a baby, Empress. You don't need to do anything. We're going to look after you.'

'How come you never hug me like that?' Aniya joked, rubbing Empress's back.

Dawn let go of Empress and stepped back. 'I went out to get you some of that lactose-free milk. Why don't you go up and have a bath and I'll make you a cup of hot chocolate?'

Empress knew she was going to cry again, so she said a quick thank you and made her way upstairs.

When Empress had bathed and was in a pair of fresh pyjamas and Aniya was in the shower, Dawn came into Aniya's room, a mug of hot chocolate in hand.

'Here we go.' She placed the mug down on the bedside table. 'It's a bit hot.'

'Thanks, Dawn.'

'You're welcome,' Dawn said. 'I've spoken to your headmistress, and I've told her what's happened. We've agreed that you'll have the day at home tomorrow, just so we can get your bedroom sorted, and you can unpack and everything. How does that sound?'

'...why are you being so nice to me?' Empress looked down at the bedsheets and started to pick at a loose thread.

'Because, Empress, you are kind, and a good girl.' Dawn smiled. 'And you deserve nothing but kindness and goodness back. It's as simple as that.'

Dawn stood up and walked to the door. 'And don't stay up talking late again with Aniya. I don't want a repeat performance of the other morning. Honestly, when you two woke up on your birthday I did not know what was going on with either of you. It was very strange.'

Empress laughed. 'Night, Dawn.'

'Goodnight, Empress.'

Chapter Seven

Two years later

'What shall we do for our birthday?' Aniya asked Empress, a cheeky smile flashing across her face. 'It's three days away and we haven't even decided. We're going to be eighteen. We can go *really* big.'

Empress and Aniya were sitting cross-legged opposite each other in the garden.

'I'm not even gonna ask what "really big" means,' Empress sighed, taking a sip of water.

'Well, I was thinking we could do another spell?' Aniya suggested, and was met with the sharpest look Empress could make her face do.

'I'm joking, I'm joking!' Aniya held her hands up. 'But, you know, that spell was still the best thing we could have ever done.'

'You're right,' Empress agreed. 'But what would we have done if we couldn't swap back?'

'I dunno. I think we would have had to run away to a foreign country and just live in each other's body forever.'

'That's not a bad plan.'

'Aniya, Empress!' Abib called from the house. 'Can you come in here for a word, please?'

Empress's heart sank. She knew this day was coming. That didn't mean she was ready for it though. For the last few months, she'd made peace with having to leave this house, this family.

They'd become her family, sure.

It had taken a long time for her to not feel like an imposter, and to stop thinking that every time Abib or Dawn spoke to her they were going to ask her to leave. But she was turning eighteen soon, and they wouldn't be legally obliged to look after her anymore. That's just how it was.

'Sit down, please.' Abib said to the girls, gesturing to the two empty chairs opposite him.

'Very serious, Dad.' Aniya laughed.

'Yes, it is.' Abib nodded. 'Please. Be seated.'

Empress and Aniya sat down opposite Abib. Empress held her breath.

'Right, so,' Abib began. 'What are you thinking about what's next?'

'What's next?' Empress asked.

'I know, it's a boring question, but it's a necessary one. You two are leaving sixth form this year, and we need to think about what's next.'

'As in, me leaving?' Empress asked quietly.

'Leaving where?' Abib asked her. 'What? And why?'

'This house. You guys.' Empress tried to find the right words. 'I— Because I'm eighteen, and—'

'No, good god! I'm talking about university, next steps in your career paths, or whatever the phrase is. I don't want either of you to leave, if I'm honest,' Abib said. 'Not ever. You're my girls. God, the thought is terrifying. I'm hoping you'll both go to university in London. But if you want to go elsewhere, I'll have to come and visit you both every weekend.'

'And he's not joking, you know,' Aniya told Empress.

'Empress,' Abib said. 'You are one of us. Maybe not in name. But in spirit, and everywhere else. And don't forget it.'

Empress breathed a sigh of relief. 'Than—'

'—And don't say thank you,' Abib said quickly.

* * * *

Their birthday morning came. There'd been no spells the night before; they'd cooked and watched a film with Abib and Dawn and stayed away from the internet, just in case one or both of them accidentally stumbled on some Latin and read it out loud.

'So, I've got a present for you,' Aniya told Empress excitedly. 'After we do breakfast with Mum and Dad obviously.'

'What kind of present?' Empress was suspicious. 'Why are you so excited?'

'Just wait and see!' Aniya said.

After breakfast, they set out in the little car Abib had bought them for their seventeenth birthday last year.

'Are you gonna say where we're going?' Empress asked from the passenger seat. *She* was the better driver, even though Aniya would never admit it.

'Just be patient.' Aniya smiled, even though she

actually felt a bit nervous.

About half an hour later, they drove past Empress's old block. She hadn't been anywhere near it since she'd left two years ago.

Sensing her friend's sadness, Aniya reached over and held Empress's hand.

'Aniya,' Empress said. 'I am very grateful for your support, but you're gonna need to keep two hands on the wheel, please.'

Aniya pulled her hand back in time to park outside a small café on the high street.

'Do you want some help?' Empress asked. 'I know parallel parking isn't your thing.'

'No. I don't need help,' Aniya lied to herself and to Empress. 'Just relax.'

'I'll be more relaxed if I get out and guide you,' Empress said, jumping out of the car.

When the car was sort of parked to the best of Aniya's ability, she locked the car.

'Come on then.' She gestured that Empress follow her.

Aniya walked into the café and Empress shuffled in behind her.

'But we just ate,' Empress said, confused.

'We're not here to eat,' Aniya said, stepping to the side to reveal Pauline and a two-and-a-half-year-old Leo sitting at a table in the corner. Pauline hadn't spotted her yet.

'I don't want you to feel ambushed, and we can leave if you want,' Aniya began.

'Aniya...' Empress sighed.

'...But Dad has been in contact with your mum for the last year. He's been helping her get herself sorted out, and has been making sure that Leo's been okay, too. Dad wouldn't have let me bring you here if he didn't think Pauline would do anything she shouldn't.'

Aniya was doing that thing where she spoke too much because she kind of knew she maybe shouldn't have been doing what she was doing.

'It's fine,' Empress said. And it really was fine

More than anything, she wanted to see Leo. She'd thought about him every single day since she'd last seen him and didn't think she'd ever lay eyes on him again, let alone be in the same place as him.

'I'll leave you to it, okay?' Aniya asked. 'I've got a few things to do on the High Street, so just call me when you're ready. My phone is on loud and I'll keep it in my hand.'

'Alright, but like, don't get robbed or anything,' Empress said. 'Keep your phone in your pocket, please.'

Aniya left the café. The tinkle of the door closing made Pauline look up. Her gaze fell on her daughter.

Pauline looked well, Empress thought. Better than she'd seen her before, anyway. Her hair was pulled into a neat bun that sat above the nape of her neck, and her skin looked clean, fresh.

Empress walked over, hoping that Leo would recognise her. When she was at the table he looked up, and something about the way he stared at her made her think part of him knew who she was.

'Hi, Mum.' Empress said. 'Or... what shall I call you? I can call you Pauline if you want.'

Pauline took a deep breath. 'Well, Mum is good for me. Even if I never was a good one to you.'

'Okay.' Empress nodded. 'So we're going straight in. I'm just going to get a drink first. Do you want anything?'

'No thanks, I've got a cup of tea.'

Empress went to the counter and ordered a tea with oat milk.

When she got back to the table, Pauline pointed at her. 'Leo, this is your big sister, Empress,' Pauline said to the toddler on her lap. 'Are you going to say hello?'

'Hello!' Leo waved at Empress. 'Big sister Empress!'

'Hello Leo!' Empress said, waving back. 'You're big now, aren't you? Last time I saw you, you were so little! You were a tiny little baby!'

Leo wriggled off of Pauline's lap and made his way over to Empress. He tried to pull himself up on to her lap, but gave up after a few seconds and held his arms out for her to lift him up.

'He must remember you. He doesn't usually go to anyone like that.' Pauline nodded. 'He's missed you.'

'Yeah,' Empress said. 'I've missed him too.'

Empress didn't really know what to say, or do. She felt overwhelmed, sure, but not in a bad way. She wasn't expecting to see her mum and brother, but it wasn't like seeing them had rocked her in a way she couldn't cope with. It didn't feel like a shock to the system, basically. It kind of felt weirdly familiar, even though so much time had passed.

'And I've missed you,' Pauline said quietly. 'For

what that's worth.'

Empress couldn't look at her mum. Instead, she looked down at Leo's hands. He was playing with the chain around her neck. The one with the "E" pendant that Aniya had bought her for her sixteenth birthday.

'Tea with oat milk?' The waitress came over to the table, steaming cup and saucer in hand.

'Thanks, that's for me,' Empress said, taking it from her and pushing it far away from Leo.

'I'm sorry, Empress,' Pauline said the moment the waitress was out of earshot.

'For which part, Mum?' Empress asked, still looking at Leo's chubby little hands. He was wrapping the chain around his fingers absent-mindedly, the gold links falling against the dimples in the backs of his hands.

'For everything.' Pauline said. 'I wasn't well, Empress. I don't think I was ever well, if I'm honest. And that's not an excuse. Well, it is and it isn't.'

Empress finally looked at her mum, staring into the eyes that were almost exactly like hers. The whites of her eyes looked brighter than she'd ever seen them. 'As long as you're looking after Leo,

Mum. That's all I care about.'

'I am now.' Pauline sighed. 'When you left, everything fell apart, proper. Social services came and took him. I don't even really remember that time. But I remember knowing that you were with better people, and that Leo was safe.'

'Why are you telling me this stuff, Mum?' Empress asked. 'Cos I'm not gonna feel sorry for you. And I think—Like, I've felt bad this last couple of years because part of me thinks I was the one who did something bad by deserting you.'

'I don't deserve you feeling sorry for me, Empress. And you didn't desert me. Leaving me was the best thing you could have done,' Pauline said. 'But I just want you to know that it wasn't your fault. It was mine. And you never did anything wrong. You were only a good girl.'

Leo put his little hands on Empress's face and patted her cheeks gently. 'Good girl,' he said, smiling up at his sister. 'Good girl.'

'And you're a good boy, aren't you?' Empress asked Leo, kissing him on the forehead.

Leo nodded and jumped off of his sister's lap, walking over to a young Black couple a few tables over who immediately started waving and cooing at him.

'Well, I'm glad you're in a better place,' Empress said to her Mum, turning in her seat so she could keep an eye on Leo.

'Me too,' Pauline said. 'And, you know, I've been in contact with Abib. He's the one who helped me get Leo back when I'd sorted my life out. My god, he's been helpful. And I know that's because of you. You've always attracted good people, Empress. It's because of who you are.'

'He's a nice man,' Empress told Pauline, ignoring her compliment.

'I knew that when he came on the block to get you,' Pauline said. 'I might not have been all there at the time, but I knew that when a Black man comes to claim a child who isn't even his, he must be a good person.'

Pauline tried not to laugh at her own joke but failed.

'I'm playing. But look – he has my address if you ever want it, and you can come and see me and Leo any time you like.'

'Are you not on the block anymore?'

'That place wasn't fit to live in.' Pauline shook her head. 'Once I got my head a bit straighter, I was eligible for a place just down the road. We've been there for about a year now! And it's clean! And warm! And the lights never go off! I've got plants and everything.'

Empress thought about it for a bit.

'Well, we'll see,' she finally said. 'I'd like to see Leo when I can.'

'You always can, Empress. Just let me know.'

Empress drank her tea while she and her mum made small talk about what had happened in the last couple of years. Only the nice stuff, though. Like Empress making Head Girl, and the holiday (her first!) she went on with Aniya and her parents. When she'd finished her tea, she knew it was time to go. She gave Leo one big squeeze and told him she'd see him soon.

He smiled at her again and pulled her down gently so that her face was level with his. He gave her a kiss on the forehead and laughed.

'See you both soon.' Empress said, leaving the café. She turned to look at Leo one more time. He was already babbling at Pauline and pointing at the cakes on the counter.

She made her way to the car and got her phone

out to text Aniya.

'You okay?' Aniya said from behind her, making her jump.

'How do you always do that?' Empress asked, holding her hand out so that Aniya could give her the car keys.

'I've always told you about our psychic connection,' Aniya said. 'You know, if you fully embraced it, I think we could do amazing things.'

Empress rolled her eyes. 'You didn't really have anything to do on the High Street, did you?'

'Nah,' Aniya admitted. 'But you needed space to talk to your mum, and I wasn't going to sit at the next table, was I? Though if you wanted me to, I would have. But I knew you didn't want me to. You haven't answered me though.'

'What was the question?'

'I asked if you were okay,' Aniya said gently.

'I'm okay, I think,' Empress said, climbing into the driver's seat. 'I'll be okay. It might take time. But yeah, I'm all good. Let's go home. I'm pretty sure there's going to be a cake waiting for us when we get there.'

They set off home, riding in comfortable silence for a while. Aniya looked over at Empress and smiled.

'Do you think you're doing that psychic thing where I can read your mind?' Empress asked. 'Cos I can't.'

'I was, you know,' Aniya laughed.

'I knew it,' Empress said.

'Well. Until we master it; happy birthday, Empress,' Aniya said to her best friend.

'Happy birthday, Aniya.' Empress said to her best friend.

ACKNOWLEDGEMENTS

First of all, I'd like to thank my editors, Eishar Brar and Aimée Felone for asking me to write this, a story that I hadn't realised I'd needed to. Thank you to Marssaié for designing such an incredible cover. Big thanks to the eagle-eyed Nazima Abdillahi for proofreading, and a very big thank you to Emma Draude and Annabelle Wright on the publicity, and Ella Chapman on the marketing. It takes so many people to make one book work, and I'm so grateful to all of you.

And thank you, always, to my agent Jo Unwin.

When I was writing Empress and Aniya, I thought about how grateful I was for the friends, and their families, who took me in. If it wasn't for them, fifteen year old me wouldn't have been safe in any sense of the word. And I wouldn't have learned about art, or music, or culture; any of the parts of me that make me who I am now. Thank you to Anya Courtman, Karin Courtman, Michael Permaul and family for always taking me in, no questions asked. Til this day, even. Thank you to Mimi and Catherine Edwards for such kindness. Thank you to Keso Kendall for being like a sister to me, and to her parents Joan and Anthony Kendall for teaching me so many things. Thank you to Becca, Ollie, Alex and Caroline O'Neill for all of the days and nights spent on Earlsthorpe Road. Thank you to Alice and Hessie Dagg for looking after me. The love I have for you all is endless.